REBOUND WITH ME

KAYLEY LORING

Rebound
with Me

This is a work of fiction. Names, characters, businesses, places, events, and incidents are either products of the author's imagination or are used fictitiously. Any resemblance to actual events, locales, or actual persons, living or dead, is entirely coincidental.

Cover design by Stacy Garcia, Graphics by Stacy
Editing by Jenny Rarden

FUNNY SEXY SWEET ROMANCE

Kayley
LORING

KAYLEY LORING

For the one I almost rebounded with,
And all the reckless hearts out there
who are having way more fun than I am.

Chapter One

NINA

"*A*re you there yet?" Marnie mumbles. "I'm hiding in the laundry room so we won't get interrupted, but I forgot to bring snacks. I'm hungry."

I don't usually talk on the phone when I'm walking around in public like the rest of New York, but I need my best friend and co-worker in my ear for moral support.

"Not yet. I'm wearing four-inch heels. I can't walk that fast."

"You *own* four-inch heels?"

"Yes. How lucky am I that I don't have to feel bad about being taller than Russell now?"

Marnie snort laughs. "Please stop putting a positive spin on this. You just found out that your boss was bumping nasties with someone else while he was engaged to you. A little hateful swearing is in order."

She has a strong point. Unfortunately, my parents raised me to be an optimist. They taught me to look on the bright side of life, to see and speak of the good in people, and to never swear out loud. Which is why I am grateful to my clucktard former fiancé, who is the principal of the elementary school I teach at, for being so courteous. He waited until the Saturday *after* the last day of the school year to come clean about falling in love with a twenty-two-year-old nanny named Sadie, whom he has secretly been boinking for the past two months. Now I have the *entire summer* to come to terms with this.

Or to put it another way—after being together for three years, the motherflorker cheated on me for two whole months, and now I get to spend my summer break hating him, regretting the last three years of my life, dreading the next school year, and considering the possibility of a job at another school. Thus, I would be leaving the Brooklyn neighborhood, co-workers, kids, and community that I love just to avoid seeing the butt monkey's stupid pointy face again.

"At least now I have the luxury of getting drunk on a weekday," I say. See—I just can't help but put a positive spin on things. It's a curse.

"Amen, sister."

"Okay, I'm here. You may fetch your snacks now."

"You need me to walk you back home?"

"Kind of. But I'll need to have both hands free to hold all my booze, so..."

"Let me know when you're home. I'm gonna eat a block of cheese now." She hangs up.

I enter my neighborhood wine and liquor store, still wearing my dark sunglasses, with my head held high. My plan is to grab a bottle of something with over twelve percent alcohol in it and get back to my apartment without making eye contact with anyone.

After spending the past two days holed up in my apartment, listening to breakup songs and eating expired pasta and cookies, it took me an hour to get ready to walk here. I did not want to risk running into my ex and his new girlfriend while looking like a hobo and scouting for booze. Hence, the armor of skinny jeans, heels, shiny straightened hair, and cherry-tinted lip gloss that is so slick it looks like I've been making out with a pan of bacon grease. I may be an inexperienced shell-shocked first grade teacher on the inside, but based on looks, I would be highly ranked in Maxim magazine's Hot 100 Most In-Denial Dumped Women Who Need to Get Drunk Fast.

I've never drowned my sorrows before, but it seems like the thing to do now. Marnie came over yesterday to bring me a shoulder to cry on, several packages of baby wipes, a juice box, and a baggie full of Goldfish crackers and carrot sticks. She's a mom. And she's the only person I've told so far about this whole scenario.

What's weird is...I haven't actually cried yet. I was angry. Now I feel numb. I figure I should go through the motions of all the breakup behaviors exhibited in movies and TV shows so I can move things along. But not one of the Taylor Swift, Adele, Rihanna, or Pink heartbreak songs have gotten to me. So my plan is to get drunk, listen to country music, and force myself to cry, even if I pop a blood vessel doing it. If "Need You Now" by Lady Antebellum doesn't move me to tears, then I will call Marnie's husband's therapist in the morning.

Or try a different kind of alcohol.

I wish I'd Googled "best alcoholic drink for recent breakups" before coming here. I usually drink wine, but I want to try something different. Something unfamiliar. Something more...virile than I'm used to. Not too sweet, not too bitter. Something that will make me feel different. Something that will make me feel *anything*.

Removing my sunglasses, I let my eyes adjust to the lighting in the store. It's twilight outside—perfectly believable that I've been out all day and just forgot to remove my sunglasses until now. The man at the cash register nods at me. I've never been to this store without Russell before. I've barely been anywhere in New York without Russell, now that I think about it. I wave at the man and try to look like someone who isn't here to grab a bottle of alcohol to take home and get drunk on by herself. As if he'd care. It is literally his job to sell bottles of liquor to people, but I don't want him to know that I'm here buying alcohol for myself.

I need to stop caring so much about what other people think of me and get a flooking life.

The bells above the door jingle in agreement as I plant myself in front of an aisle full of bottles that look like they mean business. Tonight, I'm not interested in those bottles of wine with the punny names and cute labels. Tonight, I want a bottle with a skull and cross-bones on it... Well, a cute skull and crossbones at least.

Tonight, I want... I turn my head to look at the guy who's talking to the man at the cash register. They are joking with each other with ease—that Carroll Gardens neighborhood familiarity that I just don't have yet because I've always had Russell by my side.

Speaking of sides—the view of this guy's backside is enough to drive a girl to drink. He must be a butt model. Is that a thing? The way his butt looks in those jeans just makes me want to do a little happy dance. This is the first time I've allowed myself to pay attention to a cute guy butt in three years. Russell's was perfectly decent but nothing to write home about. I would write a rave Yelp review about this guy's butt. I could write a dissertation on this guy's butt.

He's wearing a gray T-shirt and black jeans, leather boots that aren't completely laced up. Simple and casual, but somehow, he makes it look sophisticated and polished. And hot. He looks really hot. I don't know why, but it looks like he could just get totally naked in three seconds. Like the clothes are only there to keep him from getting arrested.

I also don't know why I can't stop picturing this guy naked and on top of me. I have to tear my eyes away from him. My cheeks are on fire. What is happening? I'm a first-grade teacher from Blooming-ton, Indiana—I do not have sexy thoughts about strangers in Brooklyn liquor stores. I've never seen this man before in my life, and already I'm imagining what it would feel like to have him penetrate me from different angles. The kind of guy I've never spoken to before. The kind of guy who'd never pay any attention to someone like me.

I look away and back to the liquor bottles in front of me at the exact moment that I realize he's turning toward me. My heart is racing. I feel like I'm thirteen and just spotted a cute boy at the 7-11. This is so dumb. I'm going to count to ten in French, and when I'm done, I will be as calm, cool, and collected as a French lady.

Un, deux, trois…

Oh holy *merde*. He's four feet away from me.

He smells amazing—like a spicy misty forest that I want to run through in a white silk nightgown while singing.

"You look like you could use a little help."

Oh God, that sexy voice. I can feel that voice in my panties. I glance over at him. He's grinning at me. Oh God, that grin. His whiskey-brown eyes are making me feel all warm and tingly through my center, and they should come with a warning label. But I bet every single woman he looks at the way he's looking at me right now would ignore the warning anyway.

"Me?"

He laughs. "You."

Do not say anything about him helping you by getting naked or putting his penis inside of you.

"Do you work here?"

"No, but I do know my way around liquor. Professionally. I used to be a bartender. You looking for anything in particular?"

"Yes. A bottle of something with a lot of alcohol in it." I barely recognize my own voice. It's husky. Maybe I'm coming down with a summer cold.

"Well, you've come to the right store." He was probably born with a husky voice. I bet he was a sexy baby. *What is wrong with me?*

"I usually drink wine, but I wanted to try something with a little more of an…edge?" I smirk.

I smirk?

I don't smirk.

I am definitely smirking.

He crosses his arms in front of his chest, nodding. This seems to please him. He leans toward me and looks kind of like a doctor diagnosing a patient and then says, "Okay. You want something you can mix with something else or straight up?"

"I should probably mix something with something else first. Nothing too girly or fruity though."

"Got it." He passes behind me and stands to my left, scanning the shelves. The nearness of him is electrifying. Some people have that kind of energy—especially in New York City. I've been around it. Never touched it on purpose. People like that are the third rail, and I've always stood as far away as possible from the yellow lines at the subway station. But something in this guy's eyes tells me he has no interest in hurting me. "Mind if I ask what kind of mood you're in?"

"Does it matter?"

"Oh yeah. It matters."

Oh Schmidt—he has tattoos. He has a sleeve of tattoos on his right arm.

"Um. I think I'll just get gin and tonic. Thanks, though." The alarm that's going off in my brain is cautioning my feet to step away from him, but they are not listening. They're concentrating too hard on not letting me fall over while I squeeze my things together.

"Oh hell no. G and T?" He wrinkles his brow and steps a little closer to me. "At eight o'clock in Brooklyn? Alone on a Monday night? I don't think so. Gin and tonics are for sipping on your yacht at the Hamptons while you're watching the sunset like an asshole."

"Oh, well, I guess that's what I'll be drinking tomorrow, then." I cross my arms in front of my chest and face him, wrinkling my brow, mirroring him. "I've never watched a sunset like an asshole before. What exactly does that entail?"

He shrugs. "Loafers, no socks, if you're a guy. Staring at your phone the whole time and twirling your hair if you're a girl. You don't seem like a gin and tonic type to me. Not right now, anyway. You look like you need something with a little more personality and muscle."

I finally take a step away from him. "Uh-huh. You know what... I think I'll just grab a bottle of merlot and call it a night." I start to wander toward the wine section.

He follows me, not too close. "Oh God, not merlot."

"Why? Is that what assholes drink in Miami at midnight?" Now I've said "asshole" out loud twice in one night. *Who am I?*

He releases a quick, surprisingly boyish laugh—so unexpected from a guy like him. "Not even close. What's your name? I'm Vince." He holds his hand out.

"Hi, Vince. I'm...Susan." I shake his hand. It's strong and a little bit rough, and he could do a lot of fantastic filthy things to me with that hand. *Wait—what?*

He lets me pull my hand away and shoves his hands casually into his front pockets as his gaze travels slowly down to my shoes and back up to my glossy, pursed lips. "Hi, Susan. What's your real name?"

Oh, what the heck. "It's Nina."

"Nina." He nods, accepting that answer. "Hey... How about this? There's a bar two blocks down, called Bitters. You know it?"

"Yeah, I walk by there all the time."

"I used to work there. Why don't you let me make you a drink? I think I know what you need..."

I bark out a laugh. "Well, thank you for the offer, Vince, but I'm not in the mood to get raped or murdered tonight, so... No thank you."

Judging from the look on this guy's freakishly sexy face, no one has ever foregone the opportunity to get roofied by him before. Hey, I get it. He's very attractive. I would love to stare at his face and other parts of him all night. But I also don't want to get raped or murdered.

A smile slowly spreads across his face. "Good call, Nina. You don't know me. Let's be clear about this— you can watch my hands the whole time." He holds his hands up. His strong, slightly rough, very capable hands. "I'll make sure you can see exactly what's going to be going in you before you decide if you want it or not. Sound good?"

Gulp.

"Hey, Stan!" He calls out to the man behind the counter, hands still raised in front of his chest, eyes still fixed on me. "Tell Nina here that I'm a good guy."

"Enh. He's a pretty good guy."

"Thanks a lot, Stan."

I can't help but smile. Charisma. That's what this guy's got.

He turns his head toward Stan, body still angled toward me. "If anything happens to Nina tonight, you can tell the cops where to find me. Right?"

"Leave me outta this, you."

"You got it." He smiles at me. He's got one beautiful

smile, this guy, and it fades so fast I have a feeling not many people get to see it. "What do you say, Nina? Two blocks. Neighborhood bar. One drink?"

I wrinkle my nose. "So...people *do* this? Meet in a store for the first time and then go get a drink?"

He laughs, that brief, surprised laugh of a boy being tickled, before going back to being seriously hot. "Some people. Sometimes."

I mean...I guess that sounds like more fun than drinking vodka from a bottle alone in my apartment while belting out Patsy Cline songs.

Chapter Two

NINA

"I have some conditions," I say as I follow him toward the door, past Stan at the cash register.

If Stan is wondering where the tall, serious man I'm usually with is, he certainly doesn't show it. And at the moment, I genuinely do not care.

"I'm all ears," says Vince. I assume that's his real name.

"I need to take a picture of you. To send to my friend. So she can identify you, in case you do rape and murder me."

He laughs. "Okay. But only if you get my good side."

"Do you *have* a bad side?"

"Yes. But it's more of an internal thing."

I hold my phone up and snap a picture of him as he raises his eyebrow, grinning. If that's not his good side, I don't think I can handle the better one. I close the camera app on my phone, slip my phone back into my bag, and nod. I'll wait until later to text Marnie.

"We good to go?"

"Lead the way."

He opens the door for me, placing his hand ever so gently just above the small of my back as I pass in front of him. Instead of making my knees give out, it seems to give me more confidence—which is surprising. I have a feeling this is the fourth of many pleasant surprises tonight. The first was that this guy started talking to me. The second was that he invited me to have a drink. The third was that I am actually going with him.

"Have a good night, Stan." Vince salutes him.

"Thanks for stealing my customer, you jerk."

"I owe ya one."

I wave to Stan and make an apologetic face from the sidewalk as the door closes.

It's still kind of warm, and the sun hasn't set yet. There are plenty of people walking around. It doesn't even occur to me that I don't want to run into my ex. All I can think about is how flipping flapping glad I am that I put some effort into not looking like a hobo.

A mere ten minutes ago, I didn't think I was the kind of girl who went for drinks with sexy tattooed strangers. But right now I am just putting one foot in front of the other and trusting that my twenty-seven-year-old life of being smart and safe isn't about to end—it's just going to get more interesting.

Vince walks in step with me. The two-inch space between us is both appropriate and filled with possibilities. I can see Bitters a couple of blocks ahead. A few people are milling about in front of it. I take a deep breath and a quick glance at this beautiful man who's staring at me like I'm a pop quiz and he's got all the answers in his pocket.

"So, you walk by Bitters all the time, but you've never been in before?"

"I've never really been to any bar in Brooklyn, actually."

"Really?"

A sad kind of chuckle escapes my throat. "It's weird, saying that out loud."

"You new to the area?"

"Kind of."

"When'd you move here?"

"About three years ago."

He laughs and then looks back at me and realizes I'm not joking. "Jesus. What the hell have you been doing with yourself?"

"Oh, I go to restaurants. Bar and grill-type places. I mean, I did. With my fiancé. Ex-fiancé. He's older. He wasn't into the bar scene."

For a split second, it's like the shadow of a cloud passes over Vince's gorgeous sexy face. He blinks and shakes his head. "Older ex-fiancé, huh? Now I think I know why you need a drink." We arrive at the entrance to Bitters. He reaches for the door and leans into me, so close I can feel his breath in my ear. "Welcome to Brooklyn, Nina. I hope I can show you the good time you deserve." One wink as he leans away, and I have no doubt that he can. I just wonder if I'll let him.

Bitters is not too big, not too small, not too crowded. It greets us with dim lighting and the crooning of a raspy-voiced, guitar-playing singer-song-writer whose name I don't know, but I hear him from speakers all over Brooklyn. Maybe this is the summer I'll learn the names of alternative singers and actually become cool enough to live here.

"Vince!" yells out the bartender. "You asshole! Where've you been?"

Vince raises his hand in the air. "Everywhere!"

The bartender is cute and bearded and tattooed. He tosses a dishtowel over his shoulder and saunters over to the front of the bar. They clap hands, and Vince gestures for me to join him. "Nina, this is Denny. Denny —this is Nina's first time through that door."

"Hey there, Nina." Denny grins. Denny's a flirt. "Hope it won't be your last."

"It'll be *your* last if you don't watch it." Vince points at Denny.

"Nice to meet you, Denny."

Vince leans over the counter and says something in Denny's ear. Denny looks me up and down, smiling. He nods and lifts the flip-up counter for Vince.

"Take a seat, young lady," Vince says to me. He nods at the two women at the bar who have been ogling him since we walked in, shifting his attention right back to me. "One not-too-girly-not-too-fruity drink with an edge, coming right up." He holds up a very large glass.

"Just one?" I ask. "You aren't going to join me?"

"I'm having a beer."

I give him a stern look, the kind that my principal ex-fiancé gives students when they say the wrong thing.

"I'm *not* having a beer?"

"That's another one of my conditions. You're having what I'm having."

Something flashes in his eyes, and it gives me the

kind of buzz that makes me wonder if I even need alcohol anymore.

I think I'm already drunk on *him*.

"I'm starting to wonder what I've gotten myself into here, Nina."

"We're on the same page, then."

He smiles and shakes his head as he grabs one more of those glasses.

"That's a pretty big glass."

"It's a pretty big drink."

He starts reaching for bottles on the shelves behind the bar, and I'm not the only one who's enjoying the view of his backside. Those two other women eye me with jealousy, and it's strangely satisfying. The folk-rock song transitions seamlessly to a dreamy sexy techno ballad, and my body starts swaying a little, as if it comes to bars like this and sways to music all the time.

I consider sending a text to Marnie to let her know where I am. But I don't want to take my eyes off Vince's hands, as per our agreement. He watches me watch his hands as he pours and measures and shakes and strains. The final product is blue, and the cherry garnish does absolutely nothing to make it look less devastating. He places both glasses on the counter in front of me.

"Hang on," he says. "We'll get a booth. Don't drink it yet."

"Don't worry. I won't."

He doesn't make eye contact with me again until he's finished cleaning up, clapped hands with Denny, and come around to my side of the bar. He's very focused and he cleans up after himself. I like it.

"We don't have to pay for these?"

"Nah. That guy owes me so many favors, I could drink for free for the rest of my life." He picks up the glasses and nods toward a booth. "Care to join me?"

"Those drinks look like they've got more than *a bit* of an edge."

"Looks can be deceiving." He gestures for me to slide into the booth and sits down next to me. He sits close enough for the side of our thighs and arms to touch.

I look over at him through heavy eyelids. I may be giving him bedroom eyes, and I'm not even trying. It's like my body has been waiting for this opportunity for years and it's not going to let my brain screw this up by thinking my usual thoughts.

"So what'd you make us?"

"It's called an Adios Motherfucker."

My hand immediately goes to my mouth to cover up an explosive laugh.

He raises his glass. "Bottoms up."

"Here's lookin' at you, kid." I clink glasses with him and take a sip from the two slim black straws. For a blue drink with at least six forms of alcohol in it, it tastes pretty innocuous. He watches me the whole time, removing the straws from his glass and drinking directly from it.

"Not bad, right?"

"Wow. Not too girly, not too fruity. Just the right amount of edge. Well done."

"I aim to please."

"I bet you do." *Did I just say that out loud?!*

He licks his lips and places his glass down on the table, resting his elbow on the edge and leaning languidly into it as he shifts his body toward mine. "I bet you do too."

"Hah. Couple more of these and I might."

"Oh, I think one of these will be quite enough. Take your time. Enjoy it."

"I will." My lips find the tips of the straws again, and I take my time, enjoying it while he studies me. Suddenly, I'm feeling self-conscious. I clear my throat. "You said you used to work here?"

"Few years back. Like, six years ago now, actually. When it first opened."

"You a bartender somewhere else now?"

"Nah. I just worked here and some catering jobs. It was fun but not really my calling."

"What is your calling?"

He takes another sip of his Adios Motherfucker and then drags his thumb back and forth under his lip. "Well, I guess you could say I've had a lot of callings. I was a bucket drummer when I was still in high school."

"No way."

"Oh yeah."

"Like in the subway?"

"Sometimes. Sometimes around Union Square. Occasionally Times Square. But street performers can be pretty territorial."

"How'd you get into bucket drumming?"

"I knew a guy who was doing it and it looked cool. He showed me how it was done. We made a shit ton of money. You'd be surprised."

I would not be surprised.

If I saw him banging anything, I would throw all my money at him.

"I was a handyman for a while, a house painter, a property manager, a DJ."

"Like at parties?"

"Yeah. Parties, raves. Then I became a salesman."

Oh God. I bet he was a good salesman. "What did you sell?"

"Well first I knew a guy who made a lot of money selling women's shoes at Barneys."

My jaw drops. "You sold women's shoes at Barneys?"

"Yeah. You're a size seven, right?"

"Yes. Why—do you have any size seven Manolo Blahniks leftover?"

"No, I was just trying to impress you with my ability to guess your shoe size. Impressed?"

"Totally." That's a lot of jobs. He can't possibly be over thirty.

"I'm twenty-eight," he says, as if reading my mind. "Case you were wondering."

"Why have you had so many jobs?"

He shrugs. "Just wanted to see what they were like."

That is fascinating. I've known that I wanted to be an elementary school teacher ever since I was in elementary school. It never even occurred to me to see what other jobs or lives were like. He fascinates me. Or maybe I just think he's hot. Or both. It's both. He doesn't ask me about my job history. I guess because this isn't a date and he's fine with just thinking I'm hot.

There's a pause in conversation when we're just smiling at each other, and the song that's playing fills the space with a slow, sexy rhythm that makes me sway my shoulders and hips again. He lowers his chin and his nostrils flare the tiniest bit. I give myself a mental high-five for managing to hold his gaze until he finally looks away and takes another drink.

"So what else did you sell?"

"Cars. I worked at a luxury used car lot in Queens. Buddy of mine's place. Only did that a few months. Didn't like it."

"Why not?"

He shrugs. "Didn't get to hold as many women's feet at that job. Didn't see the point."

"I would have let you hold my feet if I was car shopping." *Wow, this drink is more potent than I thought it was.*

Vince smiles. "And I would have taken you for a nice long test drive."

Wow. He did not miss a beat. Again, it doesn't make me feel intimidated. It makes me feel better about myself. Still, I think it's time I say "adios" to my Adios Motherchucker. There's about a third of it left, and if I finish it, I might actually let him take me for a nice long test drive right here in the booth.

"I'm just going to go to the ladies' room for a minute. Excuse me." *Do not say you have to tinkle.* "I have to tinkle." *Schmidt.*

"Sure."

He slides out of the booth and holds his hand out to help me up. He doesn't step out of the way when he pulls me toward him. I stand with my face one inch from his neck, afraid that if I look up at him, I'll fall backwards. And then I realize he's just making sure that I can stand on my own. "You okay to walk?" he asks playfully.

"I'm pretty sure I'm okay to fly."

He laughs. "You want your purse?" He picks up my purse and hands it to me.

"Oh. Yes, I do. Thanks."

"The ladies' room is back there past the bar."

"Got it."

I put one foot in front of the other and walk, in what I'm pretty sure is a straight line, in the direction of the ladies' room. A couple of guys who are standing near the end of the bar step aside to let me pass through them, saying "hey" to me.

I feel one of them put his hand on my elbow. "You okay there?"

I guess I'm wobblier than I thought.

"Yup. Thanks."

"Thank *you*," he says.

Some guys just aren't as good at *not* seeming creepy as Vince is.

The ladies' room has one stall, and thankfully it is empty. I pull out my phone to call Marnie. Her kids should be in bed by now, and she's probably watching Netflix with her husband.

She picks up on the second ring. "Are you home? Are you okay?"

"I'm not at home, but I might be a lot better than okay."

"What?"

"Is Dave there? Can you talk?"

"Hang on, I'll go to the kitchen." I hear her tell Dave to pause what they're watching, and I hear him tell her to grab another beer and more chips. "What's going on? What's wrong?"

"Nothing! I'm at a bar with a guy I just met at the liquor store, and I think he wants to have sex with me."

She is silent for three seconds before saying, "Nina. Go home. Now. Alone."

"Why?"

"Because you're too sensitive and you are too inexperienced. You've been attached to Russell for years. God knows why—but you need to detach from him. For real. And then attach yourself to yourself—and then attach yourself to a vibrator. And *then* you can start dating someone new."

"But—"

"Do not have sex with strangers, Nina. You can't handle it."

"I'm only talking about *one* stranger."

"Don't do it."

"Okay, but hear me out."

"Are you in the ladies' room? Is there a window? Can you climb out of it? Do you need me to send Dave over to come get you?"

"Just calm down."

"Okay, but I'd kind of like an excuse to get him out of the house. He's driving me nuts."

"Hang on. I'm sending you a picture." I text her the photo of Vince. "I'm telling you, Marn. Things are happening. There's something about this guy that I'm responding to on a level that I didn't even know I had." I look around to make sure I really am alone in this restroom, lowering my voice anyway. "My panties are completely flooded!"

Marnie guffaws.

"I'm serious! Like...soaked through. There might be

something medically wrong with me. I'm losing a lot of fluids."

"I think your body is celebrating because it never has to see Russell naked again."

"He looked perfectly fine naked."

"Oh my God, you're still defending him!"

"Did you get the picture yet?"

"Hang on." There is a pause, and then I hear her suck in her breath. "Shhhhia LaBoeuf!" She's an elementary school teacher too. "*That's* the liquor store guy?"

"Yeah."

"I think I just got pregnant."

"He's really cute, right? But I mean. I should get to know him better. Ask him out to lunch tomorrow, so we can talk more? When I'm not drinking?"

"No way. You let that guy leave tonight, and you will never see him again. New plan—you need to get back in the saddle and ride that beautiful man like a bull. Immediately."

"So it's okay for me to have a one-night stand with a stranger as long as he's hot?"

"Hey, I didn't *invent* double standards. That guy's not going to murder you. He has beautiful, sad eyes. You need to drink more and then take him to your place. Make him strip before you let him through the door, though. To make sure he doesn't have a knife on him. But I am willing to bet he's packing a long hard weapon of another kind in his pants."

"Marnie!"

"*What?* I'm serious. You should be having bathroom sex with him right now instead of talking to me."

"*Eww.*"

"Don't knock it till you've tried it."

"I just want to keep a clear head for a bit and find out more about him."

"What else do you need to know about him? Does his penis work and does he have condoms? That is literally all you need to know. You want to know what *I* found out today? I'm starting to get back fat. *Back fat*, Nina. This is what you have to look forward to. Spanx City. You're single now—go have a one-night stand while there are only two parts of your body jiggling around."

"You are crazy—you're gorgeous and I'd kill for your body."

"Awww. You used to just lie to yourself and now you're lying to me too. So sweet."

"Okay, I'm going back out there. But if Vince *does* murder me—talk to Stan at the liquor store. He knows him."

"Honey, you might black out when that guy's sperm blast catapults you into the headboard, but he'll be bringing you back to life in exactly the way you need... I need to eat more cheese."

After a pause, I say, "Marn? Marnie?"

She hung up.

Marnie sends a text of a surprised mouth-open smiley face and a baguette and a donut. And then she sends a text that says **zetywop**, because she probably put her phone in her pocket without closing the messages app. That happens a lot.

I look at myself in the mirror, rip off a piece of paper towel and dab off the lip gloss because I don't want my shiny mouth to slide across Vince's face if he tries to kiss me.

WHEN I RETURN FROM THE LADIES' ROOM, VINCE gets up, steps out of the booth, glares at the guys at the end of the bar, and puts his hand on my hip. It sends a shiver up and down my spine—both his touch and the fact that he's letting those guys know he's the only one here who will be putting his hand on me tonight. He's feeling possessive of me already. And I am fine with that.

He lets me slide into the seat, and even before I've settled myself into the booth next to him, he's staring at my mouth and grinning. He's noticed that I've removed the lip gloss, and he knows exactly what it means. This guy probably knows how to read all the signs. He's probably seen all of the signs. All of the signs that say *yes, please put your beautiful mouth on my mouth*.

His body is turned in toward me, either protecting me from the other guys or keeping me from leaving. I don't even care which. I lean back against the wall, take in a deep, jittery breath, and push my drink away from me.

"You had enough?"

"I think this motherflorker has done its job."

He laughs—not as surprised as people usually are when they hear me use my faux-swear words for the first time. "Good. You feel better?"

I smile and nod. *Oh, beautiful stranger, you have no idea.*

He is still staring at my lips and smiling. It may be my imagination, but he seems to be leaning in closer to me, in slow motion, millimeter by excruciating millimeter.

"So, what exactly do you do now? For work, I mean."

"Care to guess?"

"Please don't make me guess."

"I'll give you a hint. I'm still in sales."

"Oh shit." I cover my mouth, because it has been years since I've said the word "shit" out loud. I will have to add a quarter to my swear jar. "If you're a drug dealer, I'm leaving."

"I'm not a drug dealer. I don't do drugs."

I believe him. "Oh Schmidt. Are you an escort? Are you going to charge me for this?"

"Charge you for what, exactly?" His gaze lazily travels from my eyes to my lips, down my neck, and to a place that I'm pretty sure he can't actually see unless he also has X-ray vision. He might have X-ray vision.

"Um..." My cheeks are burning up.

"I'm just messing with you." He puts his hand on my arm and squeezes it quickly and gently before placing his hand back on the tabletop where I can see it. "You blush like a schoolgirl. I can't help it. I really seem like an escort to you?"

"I guess I wouldn't really know what an escort is like. And you don't seem like a drug dealer to me either, FYI."

"Good to know."

"So what do you sell now?"

"Real estate. Commercial. Restaurants and bars are my specialty. I'm a broker."

My mother is a residential Realtor in Indiana. I don't tell him this, because apparently we aren't sharing that kind of information. But it makes him seem a little more familiar, somehow.

"Yeah? How'd you get into that? Let me guess—you knew a guy."

"I know a lot of guys. Comes in handy. You know any guys?"

"I know a lot of six-year-old guys."

"Oh yeah?"

"Yeah."

"Sounds like fun."

"I do get to eat a lot of birthday cake. So you knew a guy in real estate?"

"I knew a couple of guys. But enough about me."

Right. It's just one night. I don't need to know where he works.

"You want to tell me why you felt the need to get drunk tonight?"

"Um..."

"Something to do with that lame ex who never took you to bars?"

"Something to do with that. Yeah. We just broke up." I sigh. "I ate expired pasta and cookies all weekend. And I even had food that wasn't expired, which was weird."

"Livin' on the edge, huh?"

"Guess so."

"Feel good?"

"Almost."

"You should feel really good. We'll have to see what I can do about that." He winks at me, and I bet if someone asked me to recite the alphabet right now, I wouldn't be able to. "You want to forget about your ex, Nina?"

I cover my face with my hands. Thinking about myself and my ex and my intentions for getting drunk is making me feel insecure all of a sudden. I don't know what I'm doing here.

"Hey."

I feel his fingertip slowly trace a trail from the V between my index and middle fingers, down the back of my hand, to my wrist, along the scalloped-edge cuff of my blouse. It sends shockwaves through my body as if his finger is touching me somewhere else entirely. I spread my fingers apart so I can peek through them. *Who are you? How did you do that? What are you doing to me?*

"You don't have to tell me if you don't want to," he says. "You don't have to think about anything you don't want to think about right now."

I let my hands fall from my face, and he takes my right hand in both of his, holding it gently with his big, slightly rough, very capable hands. My left hand, shockingly, rests just above one of his knees.

I can feel him coaxing some hidden stray cat part of myself out of the shadows. He doesn't make me feel safe so much as he makes me want to know what it feels like to not care about anything other than what he has to offer. I can see it in his eyes—he registers the exact moment that I've decided to sleep with him, even as I'm still processing it myself.

Here's a guy who knows more about the secret nooks and curves of my body than I do.

I have no idea how a one-night stand works, but I

am one hundred percent sure that *he* does, and I will follow his lead. His face is so close to mine. I am staring at his mouth and biting my lower lip. *Un, deux, trois...fuck...*

"So...what do you do *after* taking a lady you just met at the liquor store to a bar for a blue drink?"

He licks his lips and looks so earnest as he says, "I can't wait to show you."

I tilt my head up the tiniest bit.

When his lips touch mine, I ease into him and this new person that I'm becoming with such a graceful force that it feels like the only stranger here now...is the girl I used to be.

Chapter Three

VINCE

For the past half hour, this totally unfamiliar voice in my head has been saying: "Don't do this. You actually like this girl. Do not do this." Every so often I try to figure out what the fuck that voice is talking about. But now that I'm kissing Nina, I realize that a) I do actually like this girl, b) she is hotter than I thought she would be, and c) I am definitely doing this.

Her sweet lips are so gentle and receptive at first, but once my tongue starts exploring that mouth, I feel her whole body relax for a few seconds before suddenly shifting gears. She leans into me, moaning softly, grabbing on to my T-shirt with one hand and my face with the other. There's a hunger there. Something inside her that she's kept locked up for a long time. Something that I am going to help her release.

My suspicions have been confirmed—this is a woman who hasn't been kissed properly in years. Maybe ever. The fact that she's responding to me in this way is a bigger turn-on than I was expecting. I'm going to have to slow things down. Stay in control.

When she starts sucking on my tongue, I get such a rush of blood to my dick, I have to pull away from her. Her long, pretty lashes flutter, and then her eyes go wide. She's remembering where she is. Realizing what she's doing, that she barely knows me. She releases my face and shirt, covering her mouth and turning away from me.

She keeps opening and closing like some flower that isn't used to feeling the sun shine on her. I like it. I want to be the one who opens her up.

She blushes, shaking her head. "I'm not usually like this."

"Maybe you should be."

She gives me a sideways glance that makes me regret saying that. Her body language is telling me she's closing off again. So much for slowing things down. I wouldn't mind talking to her more, but it's either going to have to be stop or go-hard-and-fast-before-she-changes-her-mind with this one.

"Hey." I touch the tips of my fingers to her chin to get her to face me. "Whatever you're like—I like it."

The corners of her lips curl upwards. "You are very *convincing*, Vince." She pokes at my chest. "I think you're trying to corrupt me."

"Filthy as charged, ma'am." I lean in, kissing her cheek, her jaw, nibbling on her lower lip and then licking it. "Nina," I whisper.

It takes her a moment before she can say, "Yes?"

"Let's get out of here."

Her eyes are closed, and she's swaying like she's in a trance. "Already?"

My mouth hovers near her ear. "There are a lot of things I want to do with you, and I'd rather not do them in this booth." She smells so fucking good, and honestly, I don't much care where we are, but I push her hair to the side because I want to make damn sure she hears this: "I think we should go to your place. I want to make you come like you've never come before."

Before she can think, before she can catch her breath, I cup my hand to the back of her head and pull her in for a deep kiss. She makes a little high-pitched sound that's so cute. I've caught her off guard, but she's mine again. For the night. I can feel it. She angles her whole body toward me, even though I think she's sitting on her hands to stop herself from grabbing me. That restraint is showing me just how much she's holding back, and fucking hell, I want her to give it to me—all of it.

The palm of my hand barely grazes the hard nipples that have been pressing up against the thin little bra under her white blouse. That lacy white bra has been taunting me ever since I walked into the liquor store. I trace my fingertip along her collarbone and down to the top button that's just above her cleavage.

She bites my lower lip. Not hard but not gently either.

Well hello there, naughty girl. Come out and play with me tonight.

When I look down at her, I see her smiling. Her eyes are all lit up, and she's looking right back at me as she keeps on kissing me.

"I think you just did," she says on an exhale.

"Just did what?"

She leans in to talk directly into my ear, just like I did with her before. "You made me come harder than I ever have in my life."

Holy. Shit.

"Your place?"

She bites her lip and nods.

"Now?"

She nods again.

I make some subtle adjustments to my jeans before getting up and helping her out of the booth. She is flushed and gorgeous, and we can't get to her place fast enough. I salute Denny as we head out. He's seen me leave this place with a fair number of ladies in times past, but even he must be able to tell that this one's special.

I'M NOT EVEN GOING TO THINK ABOUT WHAT IT means that I've been holding hands with this girl for five blocks. I am not a hand-holder. But I don't want to let go of her. I keep pulling her into every empty recessed storefront to kiss her. Like we're teenagers in some European movie I'd never watch. I am not PDA guy. I don't display affection in public. I just can't wait to kiss her again.

I don't touch her at all while we walk up the three flights of stairs to her apartment. She looks back at me before putting her key in the lock. I don't know what kind of expression I have on my face, but it makes her pause for a second before turning the key. As soon as we're inside her apartment and she's closed the door, I push her up against the nearest wall. She drops her purse and keys to the ground and sighs. I lift her arms up above her head and hold her wrists, watching her squirm as she stares up at my mouth. Her lips are parted. Her lower lip is trembling. Every part of her is trembling, and it's so hot. She's tense, and her breaths are heavy and fast. She's all anticipation and hesitation and impatience, and it's so fucking beautiful.

I start by kissing her neck. She tilts her head back and her pelvis forward. Her skin is so smooth and pretty, and there's just something so clean and good about her. It's driving me wild. I slowly move my hands down her arms, to her sides. To her hips and around to her ass. I squeeze it with one hand while the other makes its way up to cup her perky round breast. She makes a little surprised animal sound that's so sweet and sexy coming from her big, swollen lips. Her arms are resting on top of her head, like she doesn't know what to do with them. She's still trembling.

Whatever confidence she had at the bar is gone for now. I'm a stranger in her apartment, and I'm guessing this is the first time she's let a stranger do this with her. She needs me to control the situation so she doesn't have to second-guess anything. And I am going to do just that.

"Take off your blouse."

I hook my index fingers through the belt loops of her jeans and watch her fumble with the buttons. I should probably just rip it apart, but I don't want to scare her. When she's finally done, I help her pull that top off and let it drop to the floor, kissing her hard and massaging her tits over the thin fabric of the lacy white bra.

Why is it so fucking sexy that she's wearing a white bra? I want to remove that thing with my teeth, but I also want to take her on a picnic and see it peeking out from a flowery sundress when she's lying on the grass under a tree. Goddammit, white bra, what are you doing to me?

She's rocking her hips and humming, and I want to do everything with her all at once, but I'm going to make this last as long as I can for both of us.

"Turn around, Nina," I growl.

"What?" She doesn't seem to understand my meaning.

I place my hands on her waist and turn her to face the wall, moving her hands up so she's gripping it while I unbutton and unzip her very tight jeans. When I press myself up against her perfect ass, she pushes back into me. I slide my hand down, two fingers into the front of her panties, and she's so slippery and wet. I let out a groan as my fingertips stroke alongside her engorged clit. She's holding her breath, and her whole body is shaking. I clutch her to me and slip one hand inside her bra, massaging her breast while my other hand rubs her clit.

"Fuck, you're so wet."

"Yes," she whispers.

"This is for me?"

"Yes."

"Just for me?"

"Oh yes."

She's starting to relax. So much so that she reaches one hand back to grab my crotch. *All right.* I slide two fingers inside her. My cock just wants to be inside that warm wetness, but it's going to have to wait. At this angle, with those tight jeans, the way she's grinding down on my hand, it's the friction that's getting her off. It's more high school than I'm used to, but she's so into it, I'll keep going until she's come on my hand if that's what she wants.

She pushes against the wall with both of her hands, tensing and releasing.

"You like that?"

"Yeah."

"You want me to keep going?"

"Yeah." Her voice is girlish but raspy. I want her to say my name.

"You want *me?*"

"Yes. Vince. Yes."

She's so close. She must have been on the verge ever since we started kissing. Was that a million years ago or thirty seconds? I don't even know anymore. I rub harder, fingers flat against her clit. She arches her back, tit pressing against the palm of my hand. Gasping, she drops her head back.

I take hold of her hair, tugging at it. Just that move is enough to send her over the edge. I feel her tense up as an electric shock goes through her, and then she's undulating, making sing-song whimpering sounds that are innocent and totally fucking porny at the same time. She leans forward and tries to muffle those sounds with the back of her hand.

"I want to hear you," I tell her. "I want to hear how I'm making you feel."

She draws in a sharp breath before crying out. The most exquisite expression of pained pleasure. She reaches back to curl her arms around my neck. I bite the flesh where her neck curves into her shoulder. She lets out a yelp, and then I hear my name and a *yes*, and it's all music to my ears.

I hold her to me, hands in place, waiting for the waves and the aftershocks to subside. When they finally do, before slowly pulling my hand out from her soaking wet panties and jeans, I say, "Was that good?"

She laughs quietly, shy and breathless again. "That was pretty good, yeah."

"Good. That was just the beginning." I spin her around to face me, pick her up, and carry her to the sofa in the living room. It looks like it's just this front room, kitchen, and a bedroom in the back. I'll save the bedroom for later.

When I set her down and start to pull off her jeans, she's got this look on her face, like...*there's more?*

I remove her shoes and stroke the arches of her beautiful feet, causing her to point her toes, and then I yank her jeans off completely. I kiss her from her ankles to her calves, tickling the backs of her knees until her long legs are relaxed and spread apart. I kiss her taut thighs while she wriggles around beneath me.

As soon as I lift my head up, she pushes against my shoulders so she can get hold of my shirt and pulls it off over my head. Tossing it aside, she stares at my bare chest like it's a prize she's just won. There's that hunger again, and I'm feeling it too. She smooths her hands all over, down to my abs, back up to my shoulders, around my biceps, and then she grabs on to my rock-hard cock through my jeans. She sucks in a breath and looks up at me, rubbing her palm up the length of my erection. She licks her lips, and fucking hell I can't look at her anymore or I'll explode.

"Take off your bra."

"*You* take it off," she replies.

"Yes, ma'am." I reach around to unhook the bewitching thing, uncovering the prettiest little tits I have ever seen.

My mouth is on them in an instant, tongue swirling around her hard pink nipples, and she's already moaning and writhing around. There's no act with this girl. She's not trying to be some version of a porn star—she's just giving herself to me. And I want her.

I *want* her.

I just fucking want her.

"Vince," she murmurs. "So good."

"I bet that fucking principal never made you feel this good. I bet he never touched you like this."

Her whole body stiffens. "What?"

I'm so caught up in licking and sucking that I don't realize what I've said until she pushes me away.

"I never told you he was a principal."

Fuck.

"What...? You must have."

"I didn't." I don't even recognize her voice all of a sudden. The way she's looking at me—covering herself —confused and scared.

It's killing me.

"Who are you?"

Fuck.

I've spent a lot of my life being mad at myself, but never before have I fucked up like this at such an inopportune moment. "Fuck." I stand up slowly so I don't pass out, because there's not much blood going to my head at this point.

She grabs a throw pillow and holds it in front of her chest, sitting up straight, not taking her eyes off me.

I start to pace back and forth like a tiger in a cage.

There is no way for me to spin this now.

I punch the air. "Fuck." I gotta come clean.

I suddenly stop and stand in front of her with my feet apart, hands on my hips.

She's backing away from me, as far back into the sofa as she can go.

I blew it.

"I'm Sadie's ex." I sigh. "Okay? Sadie? The nanny?"

Nina hasn't caught on yet.

"She used to be my little brother's nanny. And she was my girlfriend. And on Saturday she told me it was over. That she'd been seeing this principal guy for two fucking months."

I watch how her face changes as she processes what I'm saying.

"Nobody's ever cheated on me before. You know? I was so fucking mad. I was just mad. I didn't know what to say to her. I just... I hated everything. I couldn't think straight. When she left my place, I followed her. And she went to your guy's place."

Nina winces at the words "your guy." I know. He's not her guy anymore.

"The principal. When he came out, I was across the

street. And I wanted to beat the shit out of him." I start pacing again. "But I didn't. I followed him. Because I had to *do* something. Because I wanted to see what kind of guy he was. This fucking elementary school principal... And he came here. To your place."

I can tell she's still barely absorbing what I'm saying. But I know what she's thinking—*Oh. Shit.*

"I waited outside. Across the street. Pacing around, like I am now. And all of a sudden, your window opens up and all these clothes and things start flying out onto the sidewalk. And then he runs out, and you're yelling and screaming down at him."

She's caught up now. She looks horrified. Not because of me but because I saw her like that.

I stand still again, facing her. Because I want to make sure she gets this part. "I know what you're thinking, Nina," I tell her. "You think I saw you when you were at your worst—but I thought you were beautiful."

She shifts around on the sofa for a second, and I wait until she's still again before continuing.

"You were so angry. You were as mad as I was, but you were saying all this amazing shit. You were angry and articulate, and I thought...this person feels exactly like I do right now. She's the only person in the world who knows how I feel right now. But she's using words instead of fists. It was amazing."

She stares at me, disbelieving.

"Really. It was amazing to me."

She's covering her mouth with her hands, her knees bent up to her chest.

"You were all, 'you motherflorking piece of grit!' Swearing but not swearing, and it was funny and weird.

But you told him exactly how you felt, and it was great. He was being such a worthless little prick."

She blinks slowly but doesn't say anything.

She's actually listening to me.

So I continue.

"From then on, all I've been able to think about is you..."

I have never said anything like that out loud to a woman before, but I let it float around for a few seconds. I can practically hear it fall to the floor with a thud. But I keep talking anyway. "I didn't want to beat the shit out of the principal anymore. Which is good— for me. I don't need that kind of trouble in my life right now. All I could think about was...getting to know you. Getting to feel better. With you."

She's studying my face. Really looking at me. It's freaking me out, but I feel like someone's really seeing me and hearing me for the first time in...so long.

"I felt..." *Oh shit. I'm gonna say it. I can't say it. Do* not *say it.* "I felt a connection."

Blech. Who am I right now? Everyone I know would laugh me out of Brooklyn.

I can't read her expression, but she doesn't run away screaming, so fuck it. I'll just keep talking. "I didn't see you leave your apartment for two days. If you hadn't come out tonight, I would have buzzed you. Asked if you wanted to talk. I don't know."

She flinches, clutching the pillow to her chest again. "Wait... You've been watching my apartment for two days?"

"No. Not all the time. I have a job and a life. I hung out at the coffee shop at the end of the block."

She blinks. "So you were only part-time stalking me." She's not teasing me. She's trying to figure this out.

"It wasn't stalking."

"You *followed me* to the liquor store?"

"Everyone does that in New York. You see someone you're interested in when you're out, you follow her around to see what's up. That's not stalking. That's being a guy in New York."

She raises an eyebrow, not sure if she can accept this, but she lets it slide. Then she screws up her pretty face and says something that I am totally not expecting. "I don't understand. Are you still in love with Sadie?"

"What? *No.* Fuck, no."

"But are you... It sounds like you still have a lot of feelings about her."

Feelings. Yeah. I've got feelings. But I'm sure as shit not going to tell Nina about them. Not now.

"The only feeling I have about *her* is anger." My face is hot. I need to move. I should just go. Why am I even here?

Fuck.

But I can't stop talking to this woman. I don't want to stop. For the first time in so fucking long, I want to get stuff off my chest. Come clean. That's what it feels like. It feels like I'm coming clean. Because she's so clean.

I don't know.

I don't know why, but I think she can handle it.

I think she can handle *me.*

I think I *want* her to.

I can't look at her, but I don't want to leave.

I pace around again.

"You're mad at Sadie because she cheated on you," she says. "For two months. With someone so different."

The heat.

The heat on my skin.

In my blood.

It has to come out.

"It's not that, even."

"It's not?"

"No. I can't fucking believe she did this. My family trusted her. I can't believe she just fucking left us!"

I take two steps and punch the wall in front of me, and I don't even realize I'm doing it until I hear her scream.

Shit.

My fist is through the drywall.

"Shit." I pull my fist out and look over at her. "I am so sorry."

She doesn't seem scared or confused like she did when I mentioned "the principal." Right now, she just looks concerned. For me.

"Are you okay?"

Am I okay?

"What? Yeah. Good thing I didn't punch the exposed brick. It's just half-inch drywall. I didn't—I'm going to fix that. Tomorrow. I'm sorry—I can fix it. Don't hire somebody else. I'll come back and patch it up."

I cannot fucking believe I just did that.

I look back at her.

She isn't even looking at the hole I just made in her wall. Her brow is furrowed as she stares at the floor, shaking her head. She looks up at me. "So... This was

just supposed to be a revenge fuck or something?" Her
eyelids flutter when she says the word "fuck."

"No. Yes. At first—yeah. But not after I started
talking to you."

She looks me in the eyes and then down at the floor
again. After a few seconds, she watches me as she
stands up. Still holding the pillow to her chest, she goes
to the kitchen. "Stay there," she says. "I'm gonna get
something."

She disappears into the kitchen. I fully expect her to
come running out with a knife while shrieking. That's
what eighty percent of the women I've been with would
do in this situation. If I were smart, I'd go out the front
door and never look back.

But I still don't want to leave.

I hear the fridge door open and shut.

Nina comes out holding a bag of frozen peas in
front of the pillow at her chest. She walks over to me,
picks up my right hand, and places the icy bag on top of
my knuckles.

The sting of cold makes me jerk back, but nothing's
as startling as the way she's looking at me—with such
kindness and understanding. I have to look away. I have
no idea what's going to happen next. I just know that I
have never met anyone like this girl before, and if I've
blown my chance at getting to know her more, my fist
will be going through every wall I encounter for the rest
of my life.

Chapter Four

NINA

*H*ere are three things I came up with when I was trying to figure out how to get revenge on my ex yesterday: 1) Pay twenty kids to attack him with squirt guns filled with neon paint. 2) Bake him forgiveness cupcakes. Spit in the batter. 3) Be really nice to him but secretly hate him and tell Marnie that he never went down on me but he once asked me to blow him in his office after school. Trust that Marnie will tell all the other teachers.

Pretty uninspired. Vince's idea is much more elegant and fun. While I would never have come up with it in a million years and it doesn't seem completely logical to me...who am I to judge? This is my first ever one-night stand. I don't seem to care what his motives are.

Ever since I began teaching first grade, I started seeing glimpses of the six-year-old boy inside every man I meet. Vince has been all man since I met him, but when he was telling me the truth about how we were connected, and after he punched the wall, I could see it in his eyes. The six-year-old boy inside of Vince is sweet and trying to act tougher than he is. He loves his mama, and he's not going to hurt me. It's a gut feeling, but I trust it.

And, I mean...no one has ever told me they felt a "connection" before. But we do have a somewhat bewildering connection.

When I'm ninety and looking back on my life, will I regret having sex with this man tonight?

Oh.

Hell.

No.

In fact...if I had to live through three years of orgasm-less sex with a man I thought would make me feel safe, just to get to this guy who has already made me feel things that I've never felt before in the span of a couple of hours...WORTH IT.

"How's that?" I ask as I hold the bag of frozen peas on the top of his hand and wait for him to place his other hand on top of it.

"Good. Thank you."

"Can you still use your hand tonight?"

"Yeah, it's fine." He doesn't get why I'm asking. "I should probably go, huh?" he says hesitantly.

I shake my head.

I haven't had a reckless heart since I was sixteen years old and had no idea that a heart could be broken. But tonight, with Vince in my apartment and that blue drink coursing through my veins...

I do something that I never would have imagined myself doing my whole life up until now. I let the throw pillow that I've been clinging to my chest fall to the floor. The look on Vince's face as he takes me in, standing in front of him naked but for my soaking wet panties, is enough to get me over my nervousness. I grab hold of his belt, pull him toward me, and kiss him. He lets the bag of frozen peas drop to the floor, grabs my ass with both hands, and lifts me up. I wrap my legs around his waist as he carries me to the bedroom. It's almost as if there was no interlude, except there's an intensity and urgency now.

"You sure this is what you want?" he asks as he lays me down on the bed, his voice husky and low and so sexy I bet he could make me come while reading the phone book out loud.

"Right now it's the only thing I want. Just don't break anything else."

"I will try not to break your bed frame. But if I do, I'll make you a new one." He pulls me down to the edge of the mattress. "I also used to make furniture." He winks at me as he lowers himself to kiss my neck, my chest, my belly while dragging his fingers lightly down my torso. He's waking my body up in ways and places that are so unfamiliar to me, but I am fully committed to opening myself up to him for the rest of this night.

"For the record," I say, all breaths and sighs, "the principal never did touch me the way you're touching me. Or make me feel anywhere near as good."

He doesn't pause from kissing my inner thigh, but I can tell that he's smiling.

"And you've already made me come more than he ever did in three years."

"Well, darlin,' I hope you're ready for more." With a few swift moves, he removes my panties, kneels on the floor, hikes my hips up, places my legs over his shoulders, and looks down at my most private place while stroking my thighs. It should make me feel so shy and vulnerable, but he's admiring me. "Fuck, you're beautiful."

I look up at the ceiling and try to relax, but I cover my face with my arms when I feel his warm breath over my lady parts. It tickles in the most grown-up way imaginable, and I have to force myself not to giggle.

"Did he ever go down on you, Nina?"

"No," I squeak.

"Fucking idiot," he mutters. "You have the prettiest pussy I've ever seen."

When I feel his tongue on me, it sends a shock of electricity up through my center, my thighs tense up, and warmth spreads across my abdomen. He licks all the way around and then flicks his tongue at my clit, which is already so sensitive that when he licks it and then gently sucks on it, I feel myself completely losing control. I let out a little squeal as my body shakes. My response seems to cause him to slow down by pressing his thumb against my clit and rubbing it while kissing my inner lips.

"Ohhh. That feels so good." I think I say it out loud. I don't know. I try to keep still, gripping the bedspread, but my body wants to move. It feels like he's kissing me all over, even though he's just doing it down there.

He moans. "I like how you taste." He runs his hand up my thigh to my knee and back down again.

I realize that I've been slowly spreading my legs wider for him. He brings his tongue to my clit again, lapping over it and on either side, circling it delicately, and then once my body starts shaking, he nibbles and clamps down on it with his lips, sucking with perfect pressure. I arch my back and scream out, and then his tongue gets fast and rough as I come undone, writhing around. I'm so full of energy but melting into the mattress at the same time. It feels so good, my body and mind can barely process it.

I don't even know when he stopped doing things with his mouth, but by the time I've finished riding the waves of ecstasy and opened my eyes, he's standing above me, wearing nothing but a condom and a proud smirk.

Welp. That ticks off all of Marnie's boxes right there.

But holy Schmidt—there's more?! I would have liked to do something for him first, but his eyes are hooded and he looks very intent on putting his big glorious erection inside me immediately. And I am not about to stop him.

I barely get the chance to wonder how it will be possible to experience even more pleasure in one night before he's kneeling and holding himself up over me.

"You ready?"

"Mmmmhmmm." We are both well aware of how lubricated I am, so I have no concerns about whether or not I will be able to accommodate him. "You're so much bigger than anyone I've been with before," I whisper.

He groans and lowers his head like he's in pain. "Fuck, Nina. You really turn me on."

I wrap my legs around him and feel a sharp jolt as he enters me, and then I relax around the heat of his shaft as he slides in deeper. He waits for me to start rocking my pelvis before kissing my mouth and then pulling out most of the way and thrusting in. I catch my breath and dig my fingernails into his back.

"You feel so good." He says it like he's never said it to anyone before, and even though I am one hundred percent sure that he has...I believe it. It can't be possible for it to feel so good to me and not feel good to him too.

He grabs on to the headboard with one hand and hooks his other arm under my shoulder, holding me in place as he slides in and out of me. I've never had so much confidence in a man as he did this to me. It frees me up to enjoy how it feels—and it feels freaking amazing. That doesn't even cover it. It feels *fucking* amazing.

My body is relaxed and joyfully bouncing around under him. I'm thinking I could let him do this to me forever, until suddenly he changes his angle and plunges up and inwards, stimulating the depths of me and making me jerk upward and shout out, "Oh God!"

No sooner than I've gotten used to that rhythm and feeling, then he deftly flips me around so that I'm on top and he's sitting up. Kissing my breasts, hands on my waist, he guides me to bear down on him. I rock back and forth, and the pressure is heavenly. I feel an entirely new kind of orgasm coming on, but he seems intent on bringing me to the brink and then shifting gears to make this last longer.

Resting back on his elbows, he thrusts upwards. I place my hands on his pecs and watch his abs contract and release, over and over. I smile and close my eyes as I remember Marnie telling me that I should ride this beautiful man like a bull. I am, but he is the champion. I have never had so much fun or felt so sexy while having sex before. I need him to know how much I love this. "Nobody. Has. Ever. Fucked me. Like this. Before!" I try to catch my breath before continuing. "Ever ever ever!"

I look down at his cloudy eyes. His jaw is tight. His whole face is tense, like he's holding on to something for dear life. There's such strength and beauty and intensity in him, I don't know if it's what he's doing to me or just *him* that's making me feel so good, but I close my eyes again and feel warmth and electricity radiating from the center of me out to every inch and cell of my body. My head falls back, and I feel a sound I've never made before vibrating against my throat. It's the sound of complete and total satisfaction.

He somehow manages to move me around to face the headboard, on my hands and knees. He holds on to my hips, thrusting with urgency, skin slapping against skin. I didn't expect it to feel good for me in this position, *but oh wow does it ever feel good*. He grunts and makes another deep animal sound as his movements get bigger and more graceful, and then I feel him come as his whole body stiffens and releases into me.

As much as I found him strong and intense and beautiful before, the way he comes is just magnificent. I feel such a rush at being a part of it.

It doesn't matter who he was with, or who I was with before, or why he decided to do this with me.

What we just did together erases absolutely everything else.

It may not be the beginning of a relationship.

But it's the end of something that I've needed to let go of for a long, long time.

We must have both fallen asleep, and it seems we're both waking up to the sound of a phone vibrating around on the floor.

Vince, who is lying flat against my back, jolts up and looks around. "Shit." I feel him crawl down to the end of the bed and hear the jangling of his belt buckle as he picks up his jeans. I turn over to find him staring at his phone. "Shit," he says again. He slips his phone back into the pocket of his jeans. "I need to use your bathroom and then go. Okay? Family thing." He doesn't look back at me as he says it, so I don't bother answering. He disappears into the adjoining bathroom, shutting the door.

I sit up, unsure if I should get dressed to see him off, but he's out of the bathroom before I can even make a decision. His jeans are back on. He picks up his socks and boots. I'm not sure where his shirt is, but I guess he'll find it.

"I, uh... I'll come back tomorrow. To fix the drywall. Okay? I mean it."

I nod, holding the sheet up over my naked body. He starts to bolt out of the room and then abruptly stops and comes back to kiss me on the top of my head, saying a perfunctory, "That was really great. I had an amazing time." I watch him pick up his shirt in the living room and then hear him open and shut the front door.

And then silence.

So that's how a one-night stand ends?

Well, flork me.

Chapter Five

VINCE

I have left a lot of apartments in a hurry in the middle of the night, but I've never done it with a smile on my face before.

I wish I didn't have to leave like that, and I'm kicking myself for forgetting about Charlie. But I guess there would have been no good way to make my exit from Nina's place without exchanging information. No need to complicate things. But fuck. I have to go back to fix that drywall. Why did I do that? And why do I get the feeling I would have actually liked waking up with her in my arms after staying through the night?

Can't think about it now. I need to get to my dad's place, like an hour ago. The last thing I want to do is let down the people who matter the most. No matter how much I enjoyed my time with Nina. I text Michelle to let her know I'm on the way while waving down a cab on Smith Street. The driver gives me a look in the rearview mirror when I tell him I only want to go about ten blocks, but I promise him a good tip. *Asshole.*

Leaning back into the seat, I have nothing else to think about besides Nina for the next couple of minutes. I know without a doubt, from the way she looked at me, that no one has ever made her come like that before. And that makes me feel so damn good. This turned out to be the best dumb idea I've ever had. My hand doesn't even hurt the slightest bit. All those endorphins I released took care of that. I can't believe she got me a bag of frozen peas after I punched a hole in her wall. Who does that?

Nina.

Why would the principal leave a woman like that? I mean, I get the appeal of Sadie, obviously. But it's mostly skin-deep. Mostly. Nina's something else. Something fresh and real. I only got a taste of it, but it's enough to know that any guy would be lucky enough to have her. Any guy who was good enough for her, that is. Mr. Principal isn't good enough. I sure as shit wish I were.

Michelle's standing facing the door with her arms crossed, foot tapping, when I let myself into my dad's Cobble Hill townhouse. I still can't believe how nice this place is, every time I come here. The old guy made a great decision when he bought this place for Clara, even though she was such a mess. But if it weren't for her, we wouldn't have my half brother Charlie.

"Eleven thirty," she hisses. "No later than ten, you said. Should have known."

I pull my dad's neighbor in for a hug. "Michelle, my belle," I croon. She's warm and squishy, and I'm going to hug the anger right out of her.

"Oh fuck you, kid," she yell-whispers at me and

spanks my ass. "I was this close to calling your father. I gotta work in the morning, and you come back smelling like pussy, you dog." She picks up her purse. "He's in his room. *Not* asleep. Waiting for you to come home." She points her finger at me, inches from my face. "You gotta find a regular babysitter. A professional. It's been months now. I can't do this every night if you guys are gonna be out plowing every woman in New York."

"Aww, Mich. You know we only plow women in this borough."

"Animal. If I had a daughter, I would tell her to stay the hell away from you." She's grinning and her eyes are sparkling, but on some level, it still hurts to hear her say this.

"Darlin', if you had a daughter who was anything like you, I would have cleaned up my act and married her by now and you know it."

All the tension slowly melts away from her face, and when she smiles, I get a rare glimpse of the beautiful young woman that still lives inside her tired, stressed-out, sixty-year-old body. "I'm getting the hell out of here before you say another word." She shuffles toward the door. "We baked cookies—don't eat them all. Go say good night to your brother."

"Good night, Michelle. Thank you. Sorry I was late."

She waves me away and is out the door, grumbling. I honestly don't know what my dad and Charlie would do without the ladies of this neighborhood. Even when Charlie's mother was still around, they helped out with almost everything. It takes a village. At least it does when there's just us three bonehead Devlin guys trying to raise a sweet kid who deserves better.

I make my way over to the closed door to Charlie's room and knock on it softly. "It's me, buddy."

"Finally!" he says.

I open the door to find him reading in bed with a battery-operated light clipped to his book. Such a little nerd. It's hard to believe he got the book nerd gene from Clara's side, but it sure didn't come from my dad... I remember seeing a lot of books around Nina's place... But I can't think about that now.

He doesn't even look up from his book when I plop down on the edge of his bed. He's so serious for an eight-year-old boy. I'm always trying to lighten him up, but maybe he's meant to be the anchor for this family.

"Whatcha readin'?"

He tilts his book so I can see the cover. *Holes* by Louis Sachar. My brother Gabe and I can't say that title without laughing and thinking about the kinds of holes that this book is *not* about. Yeah. Charlie's the mature one in the family. "How many times have you read this one?"

He shrugs, frowning. He's mad at me for coming home late. I don't blame him. "Sorry I got here late."

"Were you with Sadie?"

I haven't told him about the Sadie situation yet. She was his part-time nanny for about a year and a half. That's how I met her. Then a few months ago, she got a full-time nanny job for some rich people's kid. Couldn't afford to pass it up, she said. She was still coming around to hang out with Charlie on the weekend, for a while, but he misses her. She was actually good with him. It was, by far, her best nonphysical quality. I don't need to see that woman ever again in my life, but I hate that *he* can't see her when he wants to. I'll tell him what's what tomorrow. Not now. "She was busy."

"With the other kid?"

"I guess." Could be true, who knows. "Come on. Book down. You gotta go to sleep. You got camp in the morning. Hey—how was your first day?"

"I liked it."

"Yeah?" He's going to a day camp for the summer. Keeping kids busy and cared for is so fucking hard—especially when school's out. I honestly don't know how people have been doing it every day forever.

"Yeah, but there are too many girls."

"Too many, huh? Any good ones?"

He wrinkles his little nose. "Some of them are okay, I guess. Rory's cousin is in it, and she keeps saying my name and laughing. It's annoying."

"Sounds like she's got a crush on you."

He scrunches up his entire face. "Gross."

"She hot?"

"Shut up." He snaps his book shut and switches off the little book light. "When's Sadie coming over?" I think he knows something's up. Kid's got a sixth sense. It's creepy.

"I dunno. We'll talk about it in the morning. Go to sleep." I put the book on the shelf under his bedside table.

"When's Dad getting back?"

"Soon, probably." My dad just started dating a woman who lives in Park Slope. She's surprisingly age-appropriate, and I think he genuinely likes her. But we all know better than to get our hopes up. He hit the jackpot once in his life, but when my mom left this earth, it's like she took all his good sense with her. All of ours, really. God bless him for always getting back up on that horse, though. I don't know if I could, if I'd been through what he has. Ever since Sadie quit, my brother Gabe and I have been trying to help out with Charlie when my dad's out so we don't have to rely on the kindness of neighbors too often.

Charlie's studying my face as he lies back on his pillow. I pull the covers up over him and mess up his hair.

"You gonna sleep here?"

"Course. What do you want for breakfast?"

"Waffles," we say at the same time.

"Okay, but we're gonna have to put a few berries on them, or broccoli, so we can pretend to be healthy."

"Not broccoli," he groans, rolling his eyes. Like he can't believe how big of an idiot I am. I wonder myself, sometimes.

"Berries it is, then. G'night, kid." I turn off the bedside lamp, and the nightlight switches on. Gabe thinks Charlie's too old to have a nightlight—but fuck him. We all need a little light in our lives. Charlie is ours. He should be able to have whatever he wants, as long as we can give it to him.

AFTER CONSUMING FIVE OF MICHELLE'S COOKIES AND two glasses of milk, I crash on the couch without washing up for the night. I want to be able to smell Nina on my fingers just a little while longer until I fall asleep. I think I might even be excited about seeing her tomorrow. I am fully aware that almost everything that led up to us having sex was all wrong. So why does this feeling I have now, and everything I've felt since I first started talking to her, feel so damn right?

Chapter Six

NINA

"The nanny left *that guy* for Russell? Is she a blind idiot?"

"Oh come on. I mean, she might be an idiot, but Russell's a handsome man."

"Sure. In a very Brooks Brothers, bring-him-home-to-meet-Mom kind of way. This guy is so hot I would keep him as far away from my mom as possible. Because she would immediately kick me to the curb and try to give him a blowjob."

"I thought your parents are still together."

"They are."

Marnie came over ten minutes ago, in her Lululemon outfit and sneakers, claiming to be jogging around Brooklyn. But I know she just wanted to check up on me. She had been texting me every ten minutes, since five thirty this morning until I got back to her. Making sure I didn't get murdered. Now she wants all the juicy details, and I'm trying to stall by claiming that I need a cup of coffee first. As soon as my timer goes off, she presses down on my Bodum French press, pours me a cup, and says, "Now. Tell me about the sexy bits."

I can't help smiling as I think about how I woke up this morning, feeling sore in places I've never been sore before, in a way that has never felt so darn good. I had lain awake, remembering last night, still tasting him in my mouth, smelling him on my skin. But I almost couldn't believe it wasn't just a dream. I had immediately checked my phone to see if he'd called or texted and then realized that we didn't exchange numbers. We didn't even exchange last names.

I can't believe I physically surrendered myself to a stranger so many times. Was as vulnerable as I could be...and I might never see Vince again. The thought had caused my stomach to turn earlier—not the fact that it happened—the possibility that it won't happen again. But now that I've had a shower and an hour to get used to the idea, I am almost complacent just focusing on how good he made me feel for a night. And how he saved me from what would surely have been the lamest breakup drinking binge ever. He turned my closed-off anger into openness, turned that into lust, and turned that into sweet satisfaction. He's a sexy alchemist. I'm grateful.

And I can't stop smiling.

"Uh-huh," Marnie replies, even though I still haven't told her about the sexy bits yet—with words, anyway.

We both collapse onto my sofa.

"Well, I already know you brought him back here, because this place smells like sex. The coffee and incense did nothing to cover it up. Nice try, though."

I put the coffee mug down and laugh, pulling my knees up to my chin.

"So I take it he had a penis and a condom and he knew how to use them?"

"Oh, Marnie." I drop my forehead to my knees, covering my face with my hands. "Oh my God." I lift my head up, but I can't look at her when I say it out loud: "He had a penis and a condom. And he had fingers and a mouth and a tongue. And his eyes. Oh God, his eyes are what really killed me."

"Yeah. That and the big hard weapon between his legs, right?"

I'm blushing. I didn't divulge much information about my sex life with Russell to Marnie. Because there wasn't that much to talk about, and also, we all work together, so it wasn't appropriate. But she's easy and fun to talk to, and I have to talk about this with someone. "Oh my God. It was so amazing."

"So the sex all happened before he told you that he had stalked you?"

"After. Well—wait. Partly after."

"That's hot. I don't know why that's hot, but it's hot. Last night, Dave and I binge-watched *Arrested Development,* made out for thirty-five seconds, and then fell asleep on the couch. I woke up in the middle of the night and his hand was on my boob, his mouth smushed up against my cheek. We literally fell asleep in the middle of making out. Your thing sounds a little more fun."

"I would love to stay in and make out while watching *Arrested Development.* That's basically my dream date."

"Please. In case I haven't made it clear yet—I'm proud of you. It takes guts to spread your legs for a total stranger. Guts and a blue drink."

"I don't know why, but I just trusted him. I mean, I knew he wouldn't hurt me. On purpose, anyway."

"Yeah. It's the eyes."

"Yeah." I cover my face again, but that just makes it worse. Because those eyes of his are all I see. And his mouth. And his chest. And his hands. And his arms. And his butt. "I kind of hope he doesn't come back."

"Why?"

"Because I'm afraid I'll fall in love with him. I don't think I could handle getting my heart broken by a guy like that."

"Awww." She pats my knee. "Sweetie."

I sigh. I've been sighing all morning. Vince What-ever-his-name-is is the kind of guy who makes women sigh. And take their clothes off. And scream while having orgasms.

Oh God.

"Well. What the hell right? What's the worst that could happen? You're what—thirty?"

I gasp. "I'm twenty-seven."

"You are?" She appears to be genuinely shocked by this news.

"Yes."

"I thought we were around the same age."

"I'm five years younger than you."

"Wow."

"Do I *look* like I'm in my thirties?"

"No. God no. You look nineteen. You've just always had a thirty-something vibe to you. Like, we always joke that you have a secret husband and five kids in Canada and you just work here during the school year."

"You do? Who's we? Is that really what people think of me?"

"Well, honey, it's not an insult or anything. You're just usually so proper. It's about time you realized you don't have to act like a first-grade teacher every second of your life."

I grin. "I said 'fuck' a bunch of times last night."

"Oh, I'll bet you did. Which *Outsiders* character is he? Dallas, right? He's straight-up Dallas Winston."

This is a game we play. Whenever we have a troubled boy in our classes, we try to figure out which character from *The Outsiders* he is. I get a lot of Ponyboys and Johnnys in the first grade. By the time they get to her fourth-grade class, they're Steve Randles.

I had such a crush on Matt Dillon and Dallas Winston when I was thirteen, but I told people that Ponyboy was my favorite.

"He was probably a Dally when he was younger, but he's got those Johnny Cade eyes."

"Right," she says, nodding emphatically. "The eyes." She pulls out her phone and brings up the picture I sent her last night.

"Sodapop," we both say at the same time.

The dreamy one.

"Yeah." She finally puts her phone back in her hidden pocket, sighing. "Sodapop."

"Yeah." I stretch my arms up and yawn, reach for the coffee.

"You gonna come for a run with me?"

"Um. I mean, I don't know if or when he's going to show up, so...I should probably hang around here."

"Can't you text him?"

My face falls.

"He didn't give you his number?"

"I don't even know his last name."

"Wow. So you really might not see him again."

I pout.

"Sorry. I'm sure he'll come back. Of course he will."

"But if he doesn't, I'm totally fine with that."

"Of course you are."

"I am."

"Just, you know. If he does come back, and if you do get involved, be careful."

"What does that mean?"

"You know. A guy like that. Just be careful."

"I don't. Marnie. How am I supposed to be careful? Wear a chastity belt?"

"Yeah. Wear a chastity belt around your heart. I think that's a Sting song from the nineties."

She hops up off the sofa and stretches her hamstrings, checks her Fitbit. "Okay. I'm gonna go. Call me if you need to talk more. Find an excuse to take more pictures of him if he does come back."

I laugh. "Um. No." I get up to hug her. "Thanks for coming by."

"One of these days you're coming jogging with me."

"Oh for sure."

"Stay gold, Ponygirl."

WHILE I FINISH MY COFFEE, I STARE AT THE HOLE

that Vince punched in the drywall. I suddenly remember that he said, "I can't believe she fucking left *us*."

Who is *us*? Does he have a kid? Or was he talking about the little brother he mentioned? There is so much I don't know about him, but I still feel like he knows me so well. How is that possible?

I wonder if he's actually going to come back. Part of me doesn't even want that hole in the wall to be patched up. I want to take a picture of it and post it on Instagram and say: ***Last night I had a hot one-night stand with a bad boy stranger, and all I got was this hole in the wall and about ninety orgasms.***

To prepare for Vince's possible return, I'm going to listen to Joni Mitchell, drink tea, and try to put together an outfit for today that says: "I have no regrets about last night; however, I'm not really that kind of girl. But thank you for honoring your commitment to filling up my hole."

Chapter Seven

VINCE

———————

I shouldn't go back. But I told her I'd go back. I want to see her again. But it's a bad idea. We don't have anything in common. But last night was hot. I can't be the guy who punched a hole in her wall, fucked her, and then left without an explanation. I'm not that guy. I'm just the guy who can't stop thinking about her, apparently.

It's probably just because she's new.

It probably just means I need to get back out there, start seeing new people.

Or it means I need to see Nina again, because last night was hot.

"Hey. You hear what I said?" my dad asks.

"What? No." I go back to buttering Charlie's waffles and ask my dad, "Hey do you have any blueberries or something?"

"That's enough butter!" Charlie cries out.

"There's never enough butter!" What kid doesn't like tons of butter on everything? I wipe the butter off the knife, onto his waffle, and put the plate in front of him. "Don't eat it until I find a berry or two. That was the deal, remember?"

"I think there's a bag of frozen berries from like two years ago."

That reminds me of Nina and her bag of frozen peas, and I don't hear a word he says again for another ten seconds. "What?"

"What is wrong with you this morning?"

"Nothing." I pull a bag of blueberries out from the freezer. It's hard as a brick. "You don't have any other fruits?"

"There's bananas."

"I don't want a banana on my waffles," Charlie complains.

"Fine. You can eat it separately." I toss out the rock-hard bag of blueberries and put a banana on the kitchen table in front of my kid brother. There. I am the best older half brother he has. No question.

"Did you get the break-even ratio to that guy for the Henry Street listing?" my dad asks.

"I cc'd you yesterday. As always. I cc'd you and Karla and Eve and Gabe."

"I didn't see it."

"Not my fault, is it?" My dad's the founding partner and CEO of the Devlin Commercial Realty Group, where I'm a vice president. So he's my boss. But it's difficult to treat him with the respect he's accorded when he's standing in front of me in his boxers and bright yellow smiley-face slippers, with a chocolate protein shake mustache and a confused look on his face.

"You hear back from the guy yet? Who's it —Briggs?"

"Connor Briggs," I tell him.

"Asshole name."

"Total asshole client. But he's very encouraged. I feel good about it. I'll talk to him and his business manager later today about his timeline. The Bushwick deal should close tomorrow."

"Good. Great!" He turns to his youngest son. "Charlie, you need to get dressed."

"But *you're* not dressed."

"I'm not taking you to camp today. Vince is."

"I am? I've got a client meeting in Williamsburg, and I have to get home to change first."

"Shit," my dad grumbles. "I've got a conference call in fifteen. We gotta get a new nanny."

"Ya think?"

"I'll have Karla get into it." He glances at Charlie and then gives me a stern look, lowering his voice. "You need to tell him. About you-know-who."

"Yeah." Might as well do it now. I take a seat next to Charlie, who's shoving half a waffle into his mouth. "Hey, buddy. There's something I need to tell you."

"About Sadie?" He doesn't look at me.

"Yeah. How'd you know?"

He shrugs. Like it's no big deal that he's eight years old and somehow knows everything.

"Anyway...you know how Sadie and I were dating? Which is why she was still coming around, even though she didn't work as your nanny anymore—I mean, she also loved to hang out with you. She wanted to see you. Everybody loves you. But Sadie and I aren't dating anymore, so you might not see her much. If at all."

He stares at his plate and chews.

"I mean, we might run into her. Or see her around the neighborhood," my dad offers.

"Yeah, for sure. But she's not my girlfriend anymore. You get what that means, right?"

He swallows and looks at me sideways. "It means you aren't boning her anymore?"

My dad slaps his forehead and groans.

"He learned that from Gabe, not me."

"It's just a matter of time before someone calls social services."

"That's not funny." I turn to Charlie, who's totally stoic in a way that breaks my heart. "Do you have any questions about what I just told you? It's okay for you to be sad or mad or whatever. You can cry if you miss her. Nobody will judge you for that."

"Well. Maybe don't cry in public."

"He can cry in public if he needs to, Dad."

"Enh. It's not like she's dead. She's just not your girl-friend anymore."

I try not to glare at him. My dad and brother think I'm overprotective of this kid's feelings because I'm such a big pussy myself. But I don't think they recognize what a sensitive little guy he is.

"If you want to be mad at me, Charlie, you be mad at me. Right? It's okay to have feelings."

"Okay." He sighs and pushes back his chair. "I have to get dressed. Who's taking me to day camp?"

My dad and I look at each other.

"Michelle?" my dad says hopefully.

"She goes to work at eight. I'll call Gabe and see where he's at."

We are *not* killing it as caregivers this morning.

———

FORTUNATELY, MY BROTHER WAS FREE TO TAKE Charlie to camp, so that somehow worked out, in the way that things always somehow do. I can't help but feel guilty, even though I know it's not totally my responsibility. I guess everyone was right when they told me not to bang the hot nanny and I didn't listen—even though her quitting to take the better-paying job had nothing to do with me. At least I don't think it did. If anything, she stuck with Charlie longer than she would have *because* we were dating. I can't believe she was the longest relationship I've ever had. The only girl I've ever dated exclusively for more than a couple of months. And how am I rewarded...?

I can't even feel angry about it right now.

Because I was rewarded with Nina.

Not that she's mine.

I was rewarded with last night.

Last night was perfect.

Well, it wasn't perfect. But it was really fucking great.

After my meeting in Williamsburg, I have about three hours free. That is, if I cancel lunch and let my partner Eve dine with our twin chef clients on her own (she will love that). So I stop by my favorite hardware store to pick up supplies and find my way back to Nina's street. I have to park two blocks away because parking in Brooklyn sucks. But it's nice out, and I can use the walk to get my head straight before seeing her again.

The restaurateur I met with this morning is a real player—a guy I hung out with a lot a couple years ago—and it's been a while since I'd seen him. He immediately listed like nine women I needed to meet. Women who'd asked him about me recently. Women he'd been with who he thought I'd like. A woman who was passing by on the sidewalk outside the property I was showing him. I finally told him, "I've been in a relationship for a while, actually." He was shocked to hear this and asked to see pictures of my girlfriend. Obviously I didn't show him pictures of Sadie. I told him I didn't have any of her on my business phone. I don't know why I said that, but I was thinking about Nina and how I wish I had pictures of her. Even though I've been seeing her face every time I close my eyes for hours and hours.

Which is nuts.

I need to just get in there, patch up the drywall, and get out. It was a one-time thing. We both got something out of our systems so we could move on from our own separate things. I need to be clear with her about that. Of course, I'm just assuming that she'd even want to see me again. I'm sure I'm not her type. Unless *guy who makes me come hard and often* is her type, but I have a feeling that was a first for her.

I wish that didn't make me smile like an idiot.

I like the tree-lined street she lives on. It's not fancy, but it feels safe. I'm sure that's why she picked it. She doesn't answer after I've buzzed her from the front door twice. I walk down the stoop and look up at the top-floor windows. The curtains are open. Guess she's not home. Guess I shouldn't have just assumed she'd wait around for me all day.

"Hey," says a sweet voice from behind me. I turn to see Nina coming in through the low metal gate, carrying a grocery bag. She's wearing jean shorts and a thin white blouse over a tank top, her hair up in a ponytail and nothing on her feet but a pair of flip-flops.

I should have parked farther away so I had more time to prepare myself for seeing her again in the light of day.

I probably have a fucking heart eyes emoji for a face right now.

I can see golden strands in her brown hair, shining in the sunlight. No makeup. Her skin's glowing in the way that surely only the truly happy and innocent can glow. Looking up at me through her eyelashes, she's blushing. She is so fucking hot and cute. I want to spend the rest of the day slowly kissing every inch of her and then make her scream my name all night.

I shouldn't have come back.

I instantly feel jealous that anyone else got to see her like this, but I've got no right to feel this way.

"Sorry—have you been waiting long? I just popped out to grab a few things."

"No, I just got here. Is now a good time for me to... deal with the drywall situation?"

"Now is an excellent time. Thanks for coming back. I wasn't sure if you would."

"I'm a man of my word."

"What a pleasant surprise."

I get a whiff of her shampoo or something when she walks by me to unlock the front door. I want to grab hold of that ponytail so bad and hear her make that gasping sound from her pillowy pink lips. I shift the bag of hardware stuff and my cordless screwdriver kit to one hand so I can take her grocery bag from her.

"Oh, thank you."

"No problem."

I gesture for her to walk up the stairs ahead of me, which I'm hoping she'll consider to be gentlemanly. But obviously I just want to enjoy the view of her perfect ass in those jean shorts.

Jesus.

By the time we get to the second floor, I have to keep my eyes glued to the stairs and run Brooklyn zip codes through my head so I don't have a pants tent by the time we get to her apartment.

When we get inside her apartment, I smell incense. She doesn't seem like the incense-lighting type, but I guess everyone in Brooklyn is that type.

She takes the grocery bag to the kitchen, opens a window in the living room, and leans against the window ledge instead of coming back over to where I'm standing by the hole in the drywall. I still can't believe I did that.

"Can I get you anything?"

"Actually, I forgot to get a drop cloth. Do you have an old towel or something I can spread on the floor so I don't mess it up?"

"I have a drop cloth, actually. For my art projects."

"You an artist?"

"No. I'm a first-grade teacher. I just fool around with paint sometimes and take my paintings to show the class. So they can feel better about their own work." She giggles.

I want to ask her so many questions about being a first-grade teacher, but I also don't want to know too much or I'll just want to know more and more. I'll just *want* more and more.

She places the drop cloth on the floor under the wall that I'll be working on, while I set out the stuff I brought. I can tell she's uncomfortable because I didn't ask her more about her job, but we're both going to have to live with that.

Her toes look so cute in those flip-flops. They're the prettiest little toes. I don't have a toe thing, but those are some dainty fucking toes. Light pink polish, clean and flawless. Shit. I'm staring at her toes. I can't stop.

She wiggles them, shifts her weight from one foot to another and back again. "Um." She bites her lower lip and sticks her hands into the front pockets of her jean shorts.

Now I'm going to stare at her thumbs like an idiot. They're such pretty thumbs. What is wrong with me?

"Yeah, I'll get to work."

"I was going to ask if I could get you anything to drink. Coffee, water, lemonade?"

"I'm good, thanks." *But I definitely should not have come back.* "I should get to it. I've got an appointment later."

"Yes. Of course. Don't let me keep you. I'll just, uhh... I'll get out of your way. I'll be in the bedroom if you need me. I mean. I'll be reading a book. In my bedroom. Since it's the only other room besides this one. And the kitchen. Help yourself to anything in the kitchen if you want. Or, you know, the bathroom's right there."

"Got it. Thanks."

She practically skips into her bedroom while I start to cut a square of drywall patch to size. I realize that I won't have time to go home to change before my next meeting, and I don't want to get dust or drywall compound on my shirt. I take my shirt off and place it on the back of an armchair, looking over to the door to the bedroom, wondering if the right thing to do is to announce that I'm taking my shirt off. So it doesn't freak her out when she sees me. But it's not like she hasn't seen me with my shirt off. It's not like her face didn't light up like a Christmas tree when she pulled my shirt off last night and ran her hands all over my torso.

Fuck.

When I stick my fingers inside the hole in the wall to check around for electrical cords before going at it with a drywall saw, I can't help but think about where my fingers were last night. Inside her. I have to tell myself out loud, under my breath, to just *be cool, for fuck's sake*.

Screwing the drywall patch to a piece of wooden board behind it should not be torture, but it is. Just thinking about the word "screw." What am I—twelve?

I can hear her yawning and shifting positions on her bed, and even though I know she's reading a book, I can't *not* picture her reading a book naked.

"*Fuck*." I mutter a little too loud.

"You okay?" she calls out.

She probably thinks I banged up my finger or something. *No, I'm not okay—I can't think about anything but you and your fucking stunning naked body.* "Yeah, I just dropped something. Sorry."

I wait to see if she comes in, but she doesn't. She is very good at giving me space. Maybe a little too good. Why isn't she hovering? Why isn't she all over me? Did I not give her as good a time as I thought I did...?

Nah. I definitely did.

Almost half an hour has passed by the time I'm spreading a piece of mesh over the drywall compound. The silence has been alternately anxiety-fueling and comforting. I like that she doesn't need my attention. It's cool. And the opposite of what I'm used to.

What's her game? I've never known a girl like her. Sadie's a bit younger, but she had game. She had us all wrapped around her finger, but she was manipulative, and I knew it. I figured she had to be a good person because she was good with Charlie. Is it possible that last night I slept with the only girl in New York who has *no* game?

Anyone would say that if I'm still comparing her to Sadie, then it is way too soon to get involved with her, and they'd be right.

I stand up and clear my throat. I don't have anything to wipe my hands on except her drop cloth, and I don't want to mess it up.

Shit, I forgot to buy paint.

I clear my throat again and call out to her. "Hey, you don't have any of the paint to match this, do you?"

"What's that?"

She pops her head out through the bedroom door, and her eyes get so big when she sees me here with my shirt off, and then she blushes and looks away. It's so fucking cute.

"Sorry, I had to take my shirt off. So I don't mess it up." I'm grinning. I shouldn't be grinning. I'm not here to flirt with her.

"No, it's fine, yeah." She stays in the doorway. "Did you say something about paint?"

"I need to paint this when it dries."

"Oh, right. I don't have the paint for this. I painted the bedroom when I moved in, but not this room. I could call my landlord to ask the color."

"You know what—if it's been a few years since it was painted, it won't match exactly anyway. It's opposite the window, so the sun would have…"

"Right, good point. I mean, I could just cover that spot with a painting. It's no big deal."

"No, I was thinking I could just paint the whole wall." It's just a three-foot-wide wall next to the front door. "I'd have to come back with the paint, though. Like tomorrow, maybe."

"I mean…you really don't have to. I appreciate you fixing it. So much. But just patching it up is fine."

She doesn't want me to come back. "Okay. Well, I gotta let the drywall compound dry, and then I'll sand it. And then you can see how it looks and decide what you want."

She nods. "Okay. Thanks."

I hold my hands up and nod toward the bathroom. "I should wash my hands."

"Oh, you know what, you should use the kitchen sink. Dishwashing liquid would be better for that."

"Yeah? Okay." I head into the kitchen. I can use her

paper towels to dry off instead of messing up her hand towel. I turn on the faucet in the kitchen sink. The sink is empty and clean, and she's got little colored glass bottles lining the window ledge above it, with single flower stems in them. Pretty and unaffected. Just like her.

I squirt the pearly white dishwashing liquid into my hands, and as soon as I smell it, I get hit with this feeling of nostalgia. So unexpected, it's almost over-whelming. This delicate, feminine scent. I realize it's the same kind of dish soap my mom used to use. Ivory soap. It's been so long since I've smelled this. I think my dad must have purposefully started using something else because he couldn't handle the memory of her every time he washed the dishes.

What does this mean? I've been in a lot of kitchens over the past fourteen years—maybe hundreds. As a Realtor, as a guy. How is it possible that this is the first time I've experienced this fragrance since I was four-teen? Or am I just *open* to noticing it now for some reason?

What the fuck is wrong with you, you giant pussy? Getting all teary-eyed over scented dish soap in some girl's kitchen? Pull it together.

Chapter Eight

NINA

*I*n the bright light of day, I now know that Vince's eyes are hazel—green, brown, *and* gold—and he is even more agonizingly beautiful than he was last night. He looked more like a professional when he first came over today, in his button-down shirt and slim tailored black pants, but there's still some kind of an edge. Maybe it was his sexy aviator sunglasses. Maybe it's just his energy. He's acting pretty detached, and the combination of that with his current state of handyman shirtlessness is almost unbearable.

I'm glad I decided to just be cool about everything. He has already turned what could have been the worst summer ever into the best, and I don't want to ruin what we had with angst and questions. Like for instance: "Why did you run off all of a sudden last night?" "Do you have a kid?" "Why don't you want my number?" "How many women does a guy have to have sex with to get to be *that* good at it?" "Did I satisfy your little revenge fantasy?" "Did any part of what you did to me actually have anything to do with me?"

But I don't need to know these things at this point. Really. I don't.

I'm just glad that he came back to fix the drywall. It says a lot about him. Although, I suppose the fact that he punched a wall also said a lot about him. I just couldn't hear it last night over the thundering sound of my surging hormones and beating heart.

When he comes out of the kitchen, wiping his hands on his abs, he has the strangest look on his face. I wait for him to ask me an important question, because it seems like that's what he wants. But he doesn't say anything. He picks up his shirt and puts it on without buttoning it up.

"Have a seat," I say, gesturing toward my sofa. I take a seat on it, leaning against the far side and giving him plenty of room to sit away from me.

He does.

He sits on the edge of the cushion on the opposite side of the sofa, but he isn't rigid. His knees are wide apart, and he leans forward to rest his elbows on them. He's so casual and comfortable in his body. It's one of the sexiest things about him, I think.

That and his mouth. And his hands and his butt and his hair and his voice and his eyes and the tattoos and muscles. And the way he smells. Okay, literally everything. Everything. Just everything.

I sigh as I look out the window. "It's such a beautiful day."

"Yeah, it is." He doesn't make me feel dumb saying such a simple thing, and I appreciate that. That is one of the many things that makes him a good salesman, I'm sure.

He's staring at my coffee table.

Oh no.

He's staring at my notebook. I can't believe I left it open.

"Can I ask you something?" he says, still looking down at the notebook.

"Uh-huh."

"What exactly did you see in that principal guy? Russell, is it?"

Phew. A non-notebook-related question.

"Oh. Hah. Well, let's see..."

"You don't have to answer if you don't want to. I'm just curious."

You want to know what Sadie sees in him. "Well, it makes more sense in the context of our school."

His eyes widen. "Oh. Right. He's the principal at the school you teach at."

"Yes."

"So... Wait, do you know Sadie?"

"Nope. The boy she looks after is a little older than my students... I know this because Russell chose to tell me about the student before telling me about this student's nanny. And then revealing to me that he had fallen in love with her while 'engaging in a sexual relationship with her.' His words."

"What a dick. Sorry. Go on."

"No, it's just...I mean, he's a handsome man and he has this air of power...of sorts. He carries himself a certain way that sort of commands respect. And he's the king around our school, so when he zeroed in on me as soon as I started there, it was... He can be very intense and persuasive when he wants something. And protective. I guess I needed that when I first moved here."

He nods, tapping at his chin. "Hunh. Interesting." I can see him trying to decide if he should keep asking me questions. And to my surprise, he does. "So your last name's Parks? Nina Parks?"

"Yeah. How'd you know?"

"It's on the buzzer."

"Right... What's your last name?"

He pauses before saying, "Devlin."

"Vince Devlin?"

"Yeah."

"That's a good name." *Hot. That's a hot name.* "Irish?"

"My dad's side, yeah. My mother's side is French. Vincent was her father's name."

"Ah, *oui?*"

"You speak French?"

"Barely. Only when I'm nervous."

"What?"

"Nothing. I count, to myself, in French. To calm myself down."

"Does that work?"

"Sometimes. Do you? Speak French, I mean."

"Not really. I did when I was younger, but it just makes me sad now."

"Oh."

"Yeah, my mom died when I was fourteen."

"Oh, I'm so sorry." He's too far away for me to reach out and touch his knee, but I hold his gaze for as long as he'll let me. "I'm really sorry to hear that."

"Thanks." He looks over at the drywall patch.

"Can I ask you something?"

He looks back at me. "Yeah."

"Do you have a kid?"

He looks so startled that I'd ask that. "What...? Oh. No. I had to leave last night because of my little brother. My half brother, Charlie. He's eight."

"Ohhhh."

"He goes to a private school."

"Oh. I teach at a public school." *I would tell you which one if you'd ask, but this still isn't a date, I guess.*

"My dad had a date last night, and I forgot that the babysitter had to leave at ten."

"Oh."

"I just got too caught up in...you." He rests his chin in his hand and smiles at me, and I die a small death for so many reasons. The smile, the thought of him with his little brother, the unbuttoned shirt...

"I have an appointment," he says. "I should probably..."

"Yeah."

I slowly reach for the notebook to close it, as surreptitiously as possible.

His eyes fall back on the notebook cover. "Can I ask you something else?"

"Yes."

"You like Joni Mitchell?"

Oh crap, he did see it.

"Um. I was listening to her this morning." *And thinking about you.* Why did I have to doodle hearts like a thirteen-year-old? Listening to her always makes me feel more bohemian and carefree, and I wrote out: **You**

are in my blood like holy wine, you taste so bitter
and so sweet, I could drink a case of you, darlin',
and I would still be on my feet, oh I would still be on
my feet...

I can't look at him, but I know he's staring at me
and smiling. "Do *you* like Joni Mitchell?" I ask.

"I heard her a lot when I was a kid. I like that song."

Why do I feel like he's read my diary? Not long ago,
he was looking directly at my vulva, but this feels so
much more intimate for some reason.

I cover my face with my hands. I feel my cheeks
burning up. This is humiliating. "Where's an Adios
Motherclucker when you need one?"

I hear his little laugh and then feel him move closer
to me, his fingers pulling mine from my face. I'm afraid
to look at him right now. Because if I do, I might never
want to stop.

He pulls my chin toward him, and I look up into his
gold-green eyes and forget about absolutely everything.

He kisses me so tenderly at first. It's different from
last night. He's not seducing me. He's letting me know
that it's okay to like him, I think.

As soon as I start kissing him back, he kisses me
deeper, and I hear the guttural sound from his throat as
I place my hand on his bare chest.

He pulls away. "I have to go," he says, squeezing his
eyes shut. "I have a meeting I can't be late for."

"Okay."

"I mean, I really don't want to go, but I *have* to go."

"I know, it's okay."

"It is so not okay." He leans in to kiss me one more
time before standing and buttoning up his shirt.

I get up to help him put the stuff back in the hardware store bag.

"I'm gonna come back and paint that, okay? It's so unfinished, it's gonna drive me nuts if we leave it like that."

"Yeah, I agree. Finish it."

He tucks in his shirt, pulls up on his belt. He kisses me again when he takes the bag and electric screwdriver kit from me. "Thank you. I'll call you later—I mean I'll come back. Tomorrow evening. No wait, that's July Fourth. I can't. Day after tomorrow, late morning. Is that okay?"

"Sure, yes."

He kisses me one more time before disappearing out my front door. And just like that, I have something to look forward to, something to dread, and about a million butterflies in my stomach.

I still have a smile on my face when my parents call to check in. They're probably a little bit frantic and wondering why they haven't gotten even one email from me in a couple of days. I don't even know how long I've just been sitting on my sofa, smiling. "Hi," I say, answering my phone, feeling perfectly ready to tell them that I am no longer engaged to the nice principal they really wanted me to marry.

They are both exactly as upset as I expected they would be. Not so much because they believed that Russell would be a perfect husband for me but because I am now "all alone in New York."

"I'm not alone. I have friends. I'm fine."

"How can you be fine?" My mom's voice is more high-pitched than usual. "You were engaged to him, sweetheart. You're in shock."

"Maybe."

"Just don't use those dating apps," my dad warns. "Mike Smith's daughter used one of those apps and ended up dating a sexual predator—this was in Minneapolis. Imagine how many predators live in New York!"

"Dad. I won't be using dating apps or websites."

"And don't go to bars to meet people! Cindy Matthews has a cousin whose daughter met a blind date at a bar in San Diego, and he ended up raping her bumhole in an alley."

"Mom! Did you just say 'bumhole?'"

"It's true—they posted about it on Facebook."

"Oh my God. How awful."

"Just don't go out alone at night."

"Daddy. I'm twenty-seven years old. You have to stop worrying about me."

"You're my daughter. I will never stop worrying about you." His voice catches in his throat. That's about as emotional as he gets, but I know he feels it.

I get it. I know my dad is picturing twenty-one-year-old me, curled up in the corner of my closet sobbing and saying that I want to die because my first love broke up with me. He'll never forget that.

I almost forget it sometimes. I totally forgot about it while Vince was doing amazing things to my body. I started to think about it again this morning when I realized that I could actually like Vince. I started to remember how it felt to be in so much pain from being left by someone I had loved without reservation. Honestly, it felt kind of good to feel something again. As much as I'd been trying to avoid it for the past six years of my life, it was like being reunited with an old friend.

"Maybe it's just a phase for Russell. You know. An early midlife crisis. We should call him. Dad can talk some sense into him."

"No! *God.* I don't want to get back together with Russell. You guys. I wasn't happy with him."

"Was he mean to you?"

"No, it wasn't that, I just... Look, it made sense to be with him when I first moved here. It felt safe, and in the context of the school, it made sense, but...it's over. And I'm glad. I'm moving on."

There is a brief pause at the other end of the line. "Okay. Just don't move on with an app."

"I probably—definitely—won't. How's Bun doing?" *Change of subject.* Bun Affleck is the rabbit that I adopted back in Bloomington, after he bit a kindergarten student. His hutch was in the garden, and it was difficult to find an apartment that would allow bunnies, but I don't think he would have been happy in a cage anyway. So my parents graciously agreed to look after him when I moved.

"Oh, the little dear. He's very...peaceful."

"You know, Nin, we're on our way to Florida to meet up with the Robinsons in a couple of days. We could stop by on the way to see you. For a few hours?" My dad sounds so hopeful.

"Oh, that's a wonderful idea! We'll just pop over and meet you for a late lunch, maybe?"

"No, that's ridiculous. I mean, I'd love to see you of course, but it's not worth it for you to take a cab from the airport just for a few hours. I'm really fine. Really."

After two more minutes of insisting that I'm fine and trying to get them excited about their trip to Florida, I tell them I have to go.

I don't tell them that I have to hang up so I can continue thinking about a boy in peace.

I need more hobbies.

Maybe I should get a summer job.

Two days without seeing Vince Devlin.

I touch my fingers to my lips. "How will we survive?"

In some parallel universe, there's a me who chose to respond to my first broken heart by being courageously reckless and falling in love over and over again. A me who trusted that I didn't feel so much about my first love that I'd run out of good passionate feelings and had to keep them tucked away for safekeeping. So that by the time I was twenty-seven and faced with someone like Vince, I could handle it.

In this one...the world, and Brooklyn in particular, is an infinitely more sexually charged and exciting place to live in, now that I know he's out there in it. But I barely remember how it used to be so easy to breathe or to have thoughts that didn't make my body tingle before I met him.

Chapter Nine

VINCE

After getting back to the office, I had put together a market demographics package for a client, filled out paperwork for another deal, had a meeting with my sales team, got on a business development call with my brother, and returned twenty calls and forty emails. The entire time I had this big stupid grin on my face and the ghost of Nina's lips on mine.

I have no idea how long my partner Eve has been staring at me through the glass wall, but I can't even pretend to not be happy when she strides in and shuts the door behind her.

"What is going on with you? Did you get back together with Sadie?"

"No. God, no."

Eve knows about the Sadie situation because we had a client meeting on Saturday afternoon, and I was still messed-up about it. But I didn't get into any of the specifics. Like how she'd left me for a practically middle-aged elementary school principal, and I followed him to his fiancées apartment and then decided to fuck her instead of kicking the shit out of him. Eve would kick the ever-loving shit out of me if she knew I'd actually planned that.

She crosses her arms in front of her chest and plops down on my sofa. "You met someone."

"Hey, did the liquor license guy get back to you yet?"

"Yes. Don't tell me you're rebounding already."

"It's not like that."

"What's it like? Do tell. I'm just kidding. I know you're not going to tell."

I love Eve like family and I'd trust her with my life, but she's still my business associate, and I have to keep some lines drawn between us.

"Is she hot?"

I grin.

"Of course she's hot. Does she live around here? Shit —it's not a client? Oh shit, fuck. Please tell me you didn't bone the twin chefs, or I will murder you."

"Nope. Not even one of them. She's not a client. Or a potential client."

"But she lives around here?"

"You're not getting any more out of me." She always manages to get more out of me. She's the only one who can. Well, almost.

"Okay, okay. Just tell me her name."

"No."

"Maybe I know her. Corky?"

"It's not Corky. Get outta here."

"Sparky." She gave me so much shit about Sadie. "Tiffany. Amber. Lola. Ginger?"

"She's not a stripper—asshat. Her name's Nina, all right?"

As soon as I hear myself say her name and feel my lips curl into a smile, I know I'm in trouble. I turn my face away from Eve, but I know she saw. I know she heard the way my voice got softer.

She has gone silent, and it's killing me.

I snap my head around to face her. "What?"

Her lips are pressed together, and her eyes are big as saucers. "Oh, honey. You *like* this one."

"Shut up. I barely know her. Shut up."

"Aww, baby." She puts her hand on my shoulder. "You finally met someone you actually like."

I shake my head. "Not talking."

"Just promise me you won't fuck her right away."

I drop my forehead to the desktop.

"Shit. You already blew it, didn't you?"

"No. Maybe. I can't talk about this with you. Don't you have to meet your wife somewhere for dinner tonight?"

"Shit fuck shit. I'm late. Call me later—we'll talk more. Just kidding! I know we won't. But call me if you want to." She's out the door, but she pokes her head back in. "Oh hey—you should bring her to my party! Not kidding! Do it!"

"It's not like that. It's just a one-time thing. *Ish*."

"Shit, she's not married, is she?"

"No. What kind of manwhore do you take me for?"

"The kind that's ripe for making a lot of mistakes."

"Get outta here. Seriously."

She gives me a concerned look. A real one.

"It's cool. It was a fun thing that happened. But it's no big deal. See you tomorrow."

She finally turns on her heel and leaves my office.

She's not wrong, though. I am in exactly the position to make a lot of mistakes right now. If Eve knew I'd punched a hole in a wall last night, I'd never hear the end of it.

I shouldn't see Nina again. What we had was perfect. I don't want to ruin it. Except I still have to paint that wall. I can't leave that unfinished. Fuck. Maybe I should just pay Carlos to do it. Send him over there with a note and flowers from me. That would be a classy dick-move.

But I don't want to be a dick to her.

Which is why I should stay away from her.

I can't even remember the last time I felt this conflicted about anything—if ever.

I stare at my phone and scroll through for a number that I haven't called in a very long time. It goes straight to voice mail, as always, and I almost hang up before the long outgoing message is over. But I don't.

"Hey, it's Vince Devlin. I know it's been a little while... It's been a long time. But if you have time soon, I think need to see you. I want to see you. I need to talk."

*D*r. Glass's waiting room hasn't changed at all in the year or so since the last time I was here. Same shitty magazines and dusty fake plants. Same feelings of growing anxiety and impending relief at the same time. I was lucky she had a cancellation tonight so I can talk to her before I decide whether or not to see Nina again on the fifth.

I flip the switch to let her know that I'm here, trying to figure out what I'm going to say, but she opens the door to her office almost immediately.

"Vince. Good to see you. Come in."

"Hey, Dr. Glass."

I take a seat in the comfy floral sofa and move the throw pillows out of the way, like always. I know she thinks I'm trying to control the situation by doing this, but I don't care. Comfy sofas don't need more pillows. Fuck throw pillows. She probably just puts them here as some kind of test. *Does the client accept his surroundings or attempt to manipulate them? What's his mood? Is he agitated or uneasy?* It's not that. Just fuck throw pillows.

I shouldn't have come.

She smiles warmly at me, her notebook and pen resting on her lap. Her blonde-white hair is a little longer than she used to wear it, and she's got lipstick on. That's new. At some point I had this idea that she and my dad should meet and date and end up together, but that would have just been weird. Some kind of projection fantasy, and it would have made things more complicated. And I don't try to make current situations more complicated just to avoid processing old buried feelings.

I don't. Maybe I did. But I'm not doing that now.

She stares at me patiently, watching and waiting. Which is infuriating. I don't have a fucking clue where to start. I can't stop rubbing my knuckles. I swear to God they haven't hurt at all since I punched the wall, until I got here.

"Been a while," she says in a totally nonaccusatory way.

"Yeah, sorry. I got busy, and things were, you know... Coasting along."

She slow-blinks and nods. "I know how it goes. You don't have to apologize. I'm always here for you when you need me."

"Yeah. Thanks."

She waits a few more seconds and then says, "So what's going on?"

My knee bounces up and down. "Yeah, I mean, it's not really a big deal, but it might be something. I don't know."

"Okay."

I stare at the bookcase against the wall, about six feet behind her. I don't know how much time passes before I finally say something. A few seconds or a minute. "What kind of dish detergent do you use?" is what I blurt out.

She doesn't even look at me like it's a crazy non sequitur. This is probably how most sessions start with guys. "For hand-washing? In the sink?"

"Yeah."

"Dawn," she says without hesitation. "For really greasy pots and pans. Ivory for everything else."

"You do? Is that pretty common? Ivory? That brand?"

"It's quite popular among women. I'd imagine."

"Why is that?"

"It's easy on your hands and it smells nice. It has a lovely, comforting, feminine scent."

"It does... So how come I've only known two women who use it? Besides you now, I mean."

She crosses her legs, leans back, and drapes her arm over the back of her chair. "Why don't you tell me?"

"I have no idea."

"Who are the two women?"

Pause.

"Okay... So, it's over with Sadie. I mean, *she* broke up with me. That's how it went down. This weekend."

"I'm sorry to hear that." She says this as though she didn't tell me five times that she didn't think it was a good idea for me to get involved with my half-brother's nanny.

"She told me that she was with someone else. Still is, I mean. For two months."

"I see... How did that make you feel?"

"Made me feel like dancing."

"Yeah?"

"No, I was mad as fuck... Sorry. I wanted to beat the shit out of someone."

"Who?"

"The guy. Russell."

"Russell? You knew the man she left you for?"

"No, I never met him. She told me his name. Russell. Never met a Russell I liked. Ever. Except Russell Crowe. I mean, I never met him, but he seems cool."

She's scribbling something on her notebook. "So you haven't had any contact with this Russell she was seeing?"

"*Is* seeing."

"She's still seeing him?"

"Far as I know. No. I mean, I saw him. I...followed Sadie to his place after she told me. And then I followed him. After he left his place. For a while."

"Tell me about that."

I tell her about that. About Nina. I only have like thirty-five minutes left, so I tell her everything, all of a sudden, in a rush of words. Feeling-words. All that shit she taught me to use back when I was just a walking container of rage. She scribbles like mad, keeps shifting around in her seat. She doesn't interrupt me at all and then waits for me to continue when I take a sip of water. Even though I can tell she's dying to comment because she keeps tapping her pen on her thigh.

"I want to see her again," I say. Because that's what all this is leading up to. This is what I want.

"To further work through your feelings of revenge toward her ex?"

"No, I just want to see her. I don't even know if the revenge thing came into play once I started talking to her."

"But you purposefully *didn't* get her number?"

"No, but I told her I'd be back to paint the wall."

"When?"

"Thursday morning."

"Okay. And when you say you want to see her again, you mean that you'd like to have sex with her again?"

"Yeah. A lot. But I've also been thinking about what it would be like to have coffee with her in the morning."

Dr. Glass's eyes widen the tiniest bit. "Go on."

"Like, after sex. After staying the night. When I walked past a restaurant today, I thought about having brunch with her there. *Brunch*. I hate going to brunch. I just had this feeling she'd like it. So I wanted to take her there."

"That's a nice thing to think about, Vince."

"Yeah, but I mean... What's next? Thinking about marriage?"

She leans forward in her chair. "*Are* you thinking about marriage?"

"No! No. Definitely not. I just met her. I mean, we're totally different. I just meant...I don't know. She's nice. I don't know why I said that."

"It's okay if you don't know what you meant. We can explore it some more in our next session."

"I guess. I think I've figured some shit out already, though. From talking to you."

"Have you?"

"Yeah."

"Is that why you came to see me? To tell me about what happened?"

I release a loud sigh. *Fucking shrinks.* "Not only. I wanted to ask your advice."

Here we go.

"Okay. It sounds like this woman you've met is very special. And I'm happy to hear that you like her. And my recommendation is that you do not see her again until you've sorted through your anger and abandonment issues."

"I don't have abandonment issues. Sadie does. Charlie's mom does."

She gives me a look, like: *Have I taught you nothing over the years, Vince?* She thinks I'm projecting all of my youthful fears of abandonment onto Charlie. And dealing with them myself by leaving women before they leave me. Whatever—maybe before. That's not what happened this time. That shows I've changed. And I really don't think I would do that with Nina. This is different.

"There are abandonment issues to be sorted through, Vince. Tell Nina that you like her but you don't want to ruin your chances for a real relationship by rebounding with each other."

"But I don't want her to be with anyone else." As soon as I say the words out loud, I realize it's true. And it's ridiculous. I barely know her.

"Vince. I'm really very pleased to hear that you've met someone you're responding to in this way. It's a positive step in the right direction. But you've just come out of your first long-term relationship. It didn't end well. You haven't processed it yet. And while I'm proud of you for refraining from punching the principal... Rebounding is a thing. It's a thing that we do because it's a lot more fun and easier than dealing with the feelings that are brought up by the end of a relationship. My concern is that rather than unpacking and working through your deepest feelings, you're merely replacing one physical act for another. Fighting for fucking."

My eyes flick up to meet hers. Every now and then she uses the f-word to make sure I'm paying attention. It works.

"Uh-huh." My knee is bouncing again.

"I'm not saying that what you're beginning to feel for Nina isn't real. I'm not trying to discourage you from being attracted to a good woman you very much deserve. I'm saying that this is a delicate period for both of you. And if you want it to turn into a real, lasting, healthy relationship, then it's better for both of you to deal with your own issues. Separately. Now, before they get tangled up in hers. Do you understand?"

"Uh-huh." My stomach sinks. I guess part of me actually thought Dr. Glass would encourage me to start dating a nice girl, as long as I keep coming to these sessions. And maybe another part of me knew she'd tell me to hold off. "Yeah, I hear you. I get it."

"It's just a matter of having patience and trusting that things will work out with her if they're meant to."

Fuck patience.
Fuck therapy.
This is bullshit.
"Yeah. I know. You're right."
She's right. I know she's right.
I shouldn't have come here.

Chapter Eleven

NINA

....

I take three deep breaths before opening the door, but it's not nearly enough oxygen to sustain me. Seeing Vince standing there in a gorgeous shirt and suit jacket, carrying a big leather backpack and a gallon of paint, is just too much for my brain and body to process. This means he is going to be removing his shirt and jacket while he paints, and I will have to hide in the bedroom, sitting on my hands, biting my lower lip, and counting to infinity in French. He grins and tells me that he brought an old T-shirt and jeans this time. I am both disappointed and relieved.

When he passes by me through the doorway, I try not to inhale his cologne too loudly. He smells like a chic conference room in the Italian Riviera, and I want him to ravage me on the table and then go for a stroll with him on the beach.

He also seems both disappointed and relieved to see that I'm wearing baggy jeans and an oversize T-shirt. But he keeps looking down at my bare feet while he sets out the drop cloth that he brought, along with the paint tray and roller.

"Can I get you anything to drink?"

"I've got a water bottle in my bag, thanks."

I can't get a read on him at all so far, and I need to stop trying to. He's here to paint a wall, and that's it. I have already removed everything from that wall so he can get to work and then leave.

His phone vibrates in his beautiful pants. He pulls it out, and when he sees the caller ID, he tells me that he has to take the call. I tell him I'll be in the bedroom, go in, and shut the door to give him privacy and to give myself a chance to remember that I am more than just a body that's having a hormone surge. I am also a brain that can't stop thinking about him. But I have to try.

I went to the Brooklyn Botanic Garden the afternoon after seeing him, which is usually the place that I go to when I want to clear my head. And I almost did. Except when I found myself in the Desert Pavilion, surrounded by phallic cacti emerging from the ground. And all I could think about was his amazing, beautiful, erect penis. I went jogging with Marnie early yesterday morning, and even though I never admitted it, we both knew that I was just hoping to catch a glimpse of Vince around the neighborhood. Maybe with a client, at a property. I didn't. I managed to refrain from looking him up online, but all I could think about was how much I wanted to. All through the barbecue at Marnie's place, I wondered what Vince was up to. Patching up someone else's hole? Patching things up with Sadie the nanny? I don't want to be like this.

I want to be able to remember him for all the

wonderful things he said and did. I don't want to agonize over when I'm going to see him again or whether or not he's seeing anyone else or if he still wants to get back with Sadie. I want to have my memory of this one hot one-night stand and a few lovely kisses, and just let it be that.

I have the Lake George trip to look forward to, and I might even take a few other little trips. There's a whole world out there! There are probably tons of guys I could be as attracted to as I am to Vince. At least two. Or one, maybe. Or maybe it would be better to *not* be so attracted to someone. I can't just go from being engaged to Russell to being obsessed with Vince. I'm sure Vince is dying to get back out there and boink a bunch of hot chicks. I mean, why wouldn't he? I just can't be one of them.

By the time I hear him call my name from the living room, I have gotten my heart rate down to a respectable level and I'm ready to say good-bye.

When I see him standing there, barefoot in his old jeans and faded black T-shirt, I look down at what I'm wearing and realize that we somehow both chose to wear the same kind of unsexy outfit for this awkward little engagement. Although I doubt very much that he'd call what he's wearing an outfit or that he spent any time at all trying to decide what to wear like I did.

"It's not dry yet, but it's a pretty good match, I think."

He's right. There's no sign of damage. This one wall looks so fresh and clean, but it still blends seamlessly into the walls next to it.

"It looks so good, Vince. Thank you."

He takes a drink from his water bottle and then puts the bottle down on the floor by his bag. He's watching me so intently, with a look of amusement on his face. I take a step back when he takes a step forward.

"You probably have to be somewhere..."

"Eventually." He takes another step toward me, and I am backed up against my armchair. He crosses his arms in front of his chest. "How've you been?"

"Fine, good, great. How've you been?"

"I've been thinking. About you. A lot."

I reach behind myself to hold on to the chair for support. "Oh yeah?"

"Yeah." He takes another step toward me. "I know it seems like a bad idea. But I think we should keep doing this."

"Doing what?"

"Rebounding with each other or whatever you want to call it. I mean, if we're gonna rebound, why shouldn't it be with each other?"

"Maybe we shouldn't be rebounding at all."

"Maybe we shouldn't call it that."

"Whatever this is, or was, Vince, I don't regret any of it. And I'd like to keep it that way."

He stands still, arms still crossed, like he's patiently discussing a deal he wants to close with an amateur negotiator.

"It's...it's like in first-grade art class," I stammer. "All the kids are geniuses with color and expression, and if you let them keep working on a painting for too long, more often than not they'll keep adding paint until they've just made a big colorful mess on paper. But if you take the painting away from them at the right time...they're all Monets and Picassos."

"What exactly are you saying?"

"I'm saying we've painted a beautiful picture. Maybe it's time to put away the canvas and be proud of what we've done."

"Yeah? I say...maybe you should see what happens after you've made a big colorful mess of things. It might be more beautiful than anything you've ever known."

Every word from his mouth pierces my heart and makes me want to back away just as much as it makes me want to jump on him.

He takes another step closer and runs his fingers through my hair, dipping his forehead to rest against mine. "You can't tell me you haven't thought about what we'd be like together."

"Of course I have." I exhale and let the fingers of one hand twist around his as my mouth is drawn up to his like a magnet.

"Don't you want to know for sure?"

I can't answer that. I already know how it will end if we keep going. I want it to end like this. With hot memories and sweet kisses.

"Just give me the summer," he says, pressing his lips against mine. "Huh? You got other plans for a hot summer fling lined up?"

I laugh. "Well, I'll have to check my fling calendar, but I think I'm free."

He kisses my forehead. "Me too." He kisses my cheek. "Let's do this." He kisses my other cheek. "You can go back to playing it safe with boring men in September."

"You are...very convincing, Vince Devlin."

"You're impossible to walk away from, Nina Parks." He kisses my neck, and I am done for.

"Just one more time," I whisper. "Let's just do *this* one more time."

"Sure. Whatever you want." He pulls off my top and drags his fingertips along the lace edges of my bra. "Where are you from, anyway?"

"Bloomington, Indiana."

"You're kidding."

"Nope."

"You're a Hoosier?"

"Yep."

"Hey," he says, kissing my neck. "Hoosier daddy?"

It takes me a minute to realize he just made a joke, because the way he's making me feel right now is so not funny.

Before I know it, he has lifted me up and carried me, over his shoulder, to my bed. When I feel his warm skin against mine, I know that he is right. It could be the most beautiful thing I've ever known.

———

WHAT'S THE LAST THING YOU'D EXPECT OR WANT TO see when you've just had shower sex with a hot guy you've only just recently met and walked out of your bedroom to get you both glasses of water from the kitchen?

My parents?

Yeah.

Same here.

Guess who I find opening the front door to my apartment. My mom pokes her head in, and I can see my dad peering around behind her. I immediately regret giving them a spare key the first time I went back home to visit them.

My hair is wet, and I'm wearing a tank top and shorts and probably a look of shame and confusion and total disbelief.

"Oh, you *are* here! I told Dad 'she's probably just in the shower.' Didn't I say that? We've been calling and texting and buzzing."

"Hi." I glance back toward my bathroom. The door is closed, so Vince most likely can't hear that I have more guests all of a sudden. I'm not sure what to do in this situation. "What are you doing here?"

They both come in and hug me.

"Well, we did a little switching up of our flights to Miami so we could come see you, sweetheart."

"Surprise," my dad says, knowing full well this wasn't a good idea. But we're happy to see each other anyway. He shuts the door and puts the carry-on bags down in the living room, away from the front door. In case someone breaks in—so the burglars can't reach their luggage right away. Because this is New York.

"Wow, that's a bold move, you guys." *Apparently* all *the Parks are busting out of their shells this summer.*

"You look good, Nina." My mom eyes me like she can see something different is going on. "Did we come at a bad time?"

In answer to her question, my bathroom door opens, and Vince walks out with a towel wrapped tightly around his waist. I am so glad I gave him my biggest towel, because—yeesh, it could have been *really* awkward otherwise.

My mother, being a residential Realtor, has probably accidentally walked in on more than one just-showered male in her day. That this is the first time she's done it in her daughter's home doesn't seem to faze her.

When Vince stops in his tracks and looks back and forth between me and my parents, it is my mother who utters the first words. "Ohhh myyy," she says in a throaty voice that is usually reserved for my father and Antonio Banderas. "Or did we come at a *very good* time?"

"Mom!"

Vince smiles and holds on to the towel. "Oh hello." If he's appalled or nervous, he isn't showing it at all. All he's really showing is his astonishing bare torso and tattoos.

"Hello," my dad says, suddenly growing a couple of inches taller.

"Um. This is Vince. He also lives in Brooklyn. These are my parents, who are stopping by on their way from Indiana to Florida. Vince came to fix a hole. In the wall. He came to patch up and paint my drywall."

"Oh. Are you a handyman?" My mom's eyelashes flutter.

"I used to be, a while ago. I was just doing this as a favor to Nina."

"Oh, how nice of you. What a good neighbor."

"It's very nice to meet you both. I'll just go get dressed and then come back out and shake your hands."

"Wonderful."

"Sounds about right," says my father, his voice as deep as Darth Vader's all of a sudden.

"My, um. My clothes are right here, so..." Vince walks past my mom to pick up his professional clothes, which are laid out neatly on the sofa behind her. "Be right back," he says, looking at me.

I'm so sorry! I mouth to him.

He goes into the bedroom and shuts the door.

"Have a seat," I tell my parents. "How much time do you have? Should we grab lunch?"

"Well...he seems very nice."

"He really is."

"Have you known this fellow long?" My parents take a seat on the sofa, and I remain standing.

"Not really." I feel like I need to just rip off the bandage. They surprised me, so why not surprise them? "Vince and I had sex today."

"Jesus H." My dad scrubs his face with both hands.

"And then we took a shower. And had sex again— and it didn't kill me! There, I said it. We're all grown-ups here. Look! I'm alive. I'm *happy*."

My mother's mouth is gaping open. "You had sex *in* the shower?"

"Linda."

"That doesn't sound very safe. What if you slipped?"

"It's a small shower stall. There's no way we could have slipped and hit our heads. Can I get you guys something to drink? Water, coffee, lemonade?"

"Please tell me you didn't meet him on an app."

"I didn't, Mom. We met the old-fashioned way. In a neighborhood liquor store."

"*What?* Nina!"

"It's fine, Daddy. He's kind of a friend of a friend. Sort of. He's a commercial real estate broker in the area, and we just...hit it off."

"You certainly did," my mother says before exploding in a fit of giggles that I can't help but join her in.

My father is not quite so amused, but he is a thousand times cooler about this than I'd ever expect him to be.

When Vince walks out in his commercial real estate broker apparel, my mother instantly stops giggling and her hand goes to her lungs, as if she's having as hard a time breathing when she sees him in it as I did. "Oh, what a lovely shirt."

"Thank you, ma'am. It's one of my favorites."

"It just complements his eyes so nicely, don't you think, Nina?"

Down, Mom. I remember what Marnie had said about why she wouldn't bring Vince home to meet her mother, and I have to cover my mouth to keep from laughing.

"Vince Devlin," he says, shaking my father's hand and looking him straight in the eyes.

"Arthur Parks. Nice to meet you." My dad studies him.

"Linda Parks. Hello." My mother studies him in an entirely different manner.

"Very nice to meet you, ma'am."

"Such a nice, firm handshake," my mother giggles.

"Devlin, eh? You a fan of Yeats?"

"I don't know." He looks at me. "Am I?"

"Dad," I say, rolling my eyes. "My dad is a professor

in the English Department of Indiana University, and William Butler Yeats is his favorite poet."

"Ah, well. If he's the guy who wrote *There once was a man from Nantucket,* then yes, I am a big fan. And I also keep all my cash in a bucket."

"Hah! He was actually a bucket drummer when he was in high school."

After a two second beat, wherein my father's face is blank, it suddenly erupts in a smile. And then a laugh. And I am just a little bit in love with this guy right now, because very few people can make my father laugh. It's pretty much Bob Newhart, David Letterman, and Vince Devlin. "You're very quick-witted. That's impressive."

"Nina tells us you're in commercial real estate. This is such a big market. It must be very exciting work."

"It is, yes. It's a family business, actually. I grew up around it."

"Oh, how wonderful. You know, I don't know if Nina told you, but I'm a residential Realtor. In Bloomington."

"So you also have a need for *closure* and *lots* to be grateful for." He winks at my mother and then smiles at my dad so he's included in the flirtation. And I think it may be one of the high points of my mother's life.

She giggles so hard. "Oh, Arthur! Another word-player!"

"We're a dying breed," my dad says.

Vince picks up his leather backpack, which he had already packed up with his stuff before we showered. "It was a real pleasure meeting both of you. I hope to see you again sometime, but I have a meeting to get to."

"Oh, I hope we can see you again too," my mother says. More to me than to him.

"Hey, I've got a question for you," my dad says as I start to walk Vince toward the door, and I brace myself.

"What's that?"

"How do you get your hair like that? All stand-y uppy? I've tried using gel and mousse, but it just gets crispy or flops back down."

Oh, Daddy. His hair's like that because your precious daughter's been running her fingers through it for hours. "You've used mousse in your hair?" I wrinkle my nose.

"Your mother suggested it."

"It's mostly just the way it's cut. Any longer it'll flop; any shorter it's spiky."

"So no product?"

"Well, I don't want to give away any trade secrets or anything, but you gotta keep messing it up while it's drying."

"Messing it up, eh?"

"Yessir. Just have fun with it. There is a putty thing that's good if you use just a little of it. I can give Nina the name of it."

"Please do."

He opens the front door and gives me a polite and very appropriate kiss on the cheek.

His eyes are a warm tea brown, comforting and energizing all at once, and I am already hopelessly addicted.

He whispers in my ear, "I left my card by your bed. Call me whenever you want. Okay?"

I nod and watch him go until he gets to the stairs, and then I shut the door and sigh. He made cheesy jokes to charm my parents *and* shower-sexed me. He is perfect.

"Well," my mom says. "Russell who? Am I right? Holy *duck*, he's handsome."

"Yes, his resemblance to me is uncanny," my dad says, straight-faced. It sends my mom and me into another fit of laughter.

"What? Just wait until I get that hair putty and an arm tattoo. You'll see."

"It's called a sleeve."

"That too."

"I'm so glad you met such a fine man so quickly."

"Yeah, it's...he's not my boyfriend or anything, Mom. Calm down."

"Oh, but I saw the way he looked at you, honey. That fella has got it bad for you."

"Okay, okay. So did you tell me how much time you have before you have to get back to the airport?"

"Not long, really." She gives my dad a look. "Actually, we came because we wanted to bring you something." She signals to my dad to get something from one of the roller bags.

"You didn't bring me a present, did you?"

"Not exactly."

My father carefully places a small box on the coffee table in front of me and then gently pats the lid of the box.

I stare at it, suddenly feeling a little sick. "What is it?"

"It's Bun Affleck," says my mom. "His ashes. He died six months ago. We didn't tell you because we didn't want to upset you. You'd just gotten engaged, and you seemed so happy."

I cover my mouth. I don't even know how to feel. "He *died* and you didn't tell me?"

"He wasn't sick or anything. He just died of old age while he was sleeping."

"We had him cremated at that place that did Sully. They're very nice. There's a little card inside with the crossing the rainbow bridge poem. He had a very nice long little life."

I shake my head. I will deal with my feelings about the death of my bunny rabbit later. Right now, I just can't believe my parents think I'm so fragile that they can't even give me news about my pet's passing. It's ludicrous. I don't want to think of myself as fragile, either. I don't want to be so protective of my own heart anymore.

On my way back to Brooklyn, after seeing my parents off at JFK, I pull Vince's business card out from my purse. **Devlin Commercial Realty Group, Vice President, Investment Sales**

He looks almost as good on paper as he does in a towel.

I put the number in my phone and send him a text.

ME: Hi. It's Nina. My parents are gone. My dad wants the name of that hair product. When can I see you again?

Chapter Twelve

NINA

I don't know if Vince Devlin is a Catholic or not, but I have started thinking of him as St. Vince, patron saint of *girls who haven't had enough fun in their lives yet.*

I'm lying here on his big amazing bed, in his big amazing loft in a very cool neighborhood called DUMBO, watching him plate the dinner that he just had delivered. My body is both ravaged and revitalized, my brain carefree and racing. It's probably because he plowed away at me until I was hanging upside-down off the edge of the mattress.

When he had called to tell me that he'd be coming to pick me up to bring me to his place, I thought he meant in an Uber. He didn't. When I came down from my apartment, I found him casually leaning against a motorcycle, a helmet resting between his arm and hip. Every fantasy I'd ever had of Maxwell Caulfield from *Grease 2* had done nothing to prepare me for the reality of such holy hotness.

"You're kidding, right?" I said.

"Would I kid you?" He kissed me and then grinned as he handed me the helmet. "I won't go very fast, don't worry. But it's easier than driving from here to DUMBO."

I can't say that it was on my bucket list to ride on the back of a motorcycle, with my arms clasped tight around the waist of a sexy man and a warm summer night breeze through my hair...but now that I've done it, it is way at the top of my list of things that I am so glad I finally did.

His loft is beautiful and warm in a masculine way, and it smells like him. There is one huge stylish fiddle-leaf fig tree in a corner, leaning toward the light of the oversize industrial window that looks out over the rooftop of a smaller renovated factory/loft building. His living room furniture is spare but exquisite and comfortable. Next to the antique leather sofa are five plastic buckets, one much smaller than the other four. Four of them are overturned; one is a container for drumsticks.

"Is the little bucket for your little brother?"

"What's that?" he asks, all chipper as he brings two plates and silverware over to the bed. He is shirtless and wearing only a pair of sweatpants and Vans.

"Those are for bucket drumming, right? Is the little one for your brother?"

"Why yes, it is. You wanna try?"

"Uhh, maybe later."

"You ever seen someone bucket drumming?"

"In the subway station once, yeah. It was so awesome."

"I wonder if I know the guy." He puts the plates down on top of the sheet.

"We're eating in bed?"

He waggles his eyebrows. "Second course of the night."

I shake my head, feeling my cheeks get warm. "So you've given lessons to kids?"

"Yeah, why? You want me to teach your class sometime?"

The thought of him doing anything for me after September makes me excited and nervous and sad, but I just shrug my shoulders. "I mean, I'm sure the parents will hate me if I introduce my students to bucket drumming, but I know the kids would love it."

"Yeah, they would. I'm kind of awesome, myself."

"I believe you."

"Well, don't just take my word for it." He strides over to pick out a pair of drumsticks from one bucket, twirling one of the sticks between his fingers while he uses one bucket as a stool and brings another between his feet. Then he pulls two more buckets in front of that one.

I sit up, covering myself with the sheet, careful not to disturb the plates of food.

Slouching, he taps on the edge of the bucket between his legs, warming up, and then starts into a beat. He's using his feet to move the bucket in different angles and banging on all three buckets, including the one that has a bunch of sticks in it. It's not just the primal energy and rhythm or the fascinating way that he manipulates the buckets to change the sounds, or the muscles and veins that are bulging on his arms. It's the easy physicality of the performance, the confidence and focus with which he makes this noisy music—every cell of my body is vibrating because of him.

After the finale, after playing for about ninety amazing seconds, he tosses one of the sticks up in the air and then catches it. There wasn't any doubt in my mind before, but now I know for a fact that he is way too cool to be hanging out with the likes of me. My heart is pounding, and there's no way that I can digest food after that. I slowly place the plates on the floor so they won't fall off the bed...

"Wow. Where's my purse? You can just have all of my cash. That was incredible."

"That one was on the house."

When he saunters back over to me, he is only slightly out of breath and completely capable of taking mine away again as he pulls down the sheet I was using to cover myself and presses himself down on top of me.

WHEN WE FINALLY GET AROUND TO EATING DINNER, it is room temperature, but we have worked up too much of an appetite to care.

I watch him eat, like an athlete after a game. He has so much energy, but he usually seems so cool and controlled. I can't help but wonder if any of it's an act, but he always seems so authentic. Maybe that's why he's such a good salesman. I want to ask him, but I don't. I want to ask him if there's anything he *can't* do, but I don't. I want to ask him if he's ever been a butt model, but I don't. Instead, what comes out of my mouth is: "Has Sadie been in touch with you since the weekend?"

A deep crease forms between his brows as he shakes his head. "No. I blocked her on my phone, and she hasn't emailed me or anything. Why? The principal been in touch with you?"

"No. Not since I tossed his clothes out my window and yelled at him. He would see that as encouraging my bad behavior."

Vince rolls his eyes. "Whatever."

I do love that Vince is so uncritical of my freak-out that day. Whether he was watching from across the street or not. I was deeply ashamed of myself because I was still seeing myself through Russell's eyes. It's a lot easier to feel good when I look at myself through Vince's. I just can't imagine why Sadie would want to walk away from that.

"Did you love her?" I whisper.

He freezes for a moment before going back to chewing and swallowing what he was eating. He wipes his mouth with a napkin and angles himself so that he's facing me square-on. I wipe my fingers and get ready for his answer because I can tell it's not going to be a flippant one.

"I've thought about this a lot. Almost as much as I've thought about you, since last Saturday. I thought I loved her at first. I guess I wanted to. That feeling I had in my gut, I thought it meant I was in love with her because I was afraid of it. But I think my gut just knew it was wrong and I was trying to justify the choice that I'd made to be with her. Now...I think I loved who I was trying to be, when I was her boyfriend. Does that make sense?"

"Oh my God." I push my plate aside and hold my hands up over my head. "That's it." I reach out to pat his knee. "That's exactly it! I've been trying to articulate how it was for me with Russell—and that's it. I loved the person I was trying to be when I was with him. But that's not me... No, that's not true. That's always going to be part of me. It's how I was raised. But it's not who I am."

"So why were you engaged to him? I mean, you could have said no."

I curl my legs up into my chest. "Yeah, I guess. I think I'd just given up on love and it seemed like since it all happened so easily that it was right and fine and why not?"

"You gave up on it? You're what...twenty-seven?"

"Yeah. Is that one of your party tricks? Like guessing shoe sizes?"

"Hey, I don't guess. I have a gift."

"Right. You have soooo many gifts... No, I just... Well, I fell in love with my first boyfriend when I was sixteen."

"Oh." He seems surprised or maybe disheartened to hear this. "In Bloomington?"

"Yep. And it was first love, you know. It felt so big and beautiful and forever, and I thought I was so lucky to have met the person I'd spend the rest of my life with when I was in high school. And we went to IU together. I studied education, and he studied creative writing." I look up at Vince's face, and his expression and body language is so puzzling to me. It's like he's ever so slowly deflating. "Anyway, after we graduated, he decided to move to LA to be a screenwriter, and he didn't want me to go with him."

He wrinkles up his face. "Without discussing it first?"

"Not really. We had always talked about staying in Bloomington. I'd teach and he'd self-publish books until he got a publishing deal. And then he just...told me. He had already made all the plans to go out there on his own." I know what Vince is thinking. "I really don't think it had anything to do with another girl. It was just that he wanted to start over without me. And I took it really hard. And I didn't want to get hurt like that again."

"Have you seen him since then?"

"No. Not at all. He sent me an email when he got there, and I didn't write back. That was it. I got off Facebook because I didn't want to see any pictures of him or know what he was doing."

"So...you're still not over your first love?"

"I don't know if anyone ever really gets over their first love. Do they? It's not the *person* I had trouble getting over. It was being in love for the first time. And then, finding out that you can fall out of love. Or maybe I'm just an overly sensitive big baby... I've just never been cheated on before. I don't think."

"Me neither. That's the part of all this that I can't wrap my head around. I can't believe I was so busy *not* paying attention to her at that point that I didn't see any signs. I can't believe she cheated on me with *that* guy. I can't believe that guy would cheat on *you* with anyone."

"Even her?"

"Especially her. Have you seen her?"

"No. I don't think I want to."

"Yeah, it's probably for the best."

Uh-oh. I do not want to know what that means.

He lies down across the mattress, as if this conversation has exhausted him. I reach out to touch his hand. He plays with my fingers, before saying, "At least you've been in love."

"You haven't?"

He shakes his head. "Not yet." He presses his hand up against mine. "I may be an *in*sensitive big baby."

I lie down beside him. "I think you're so much more than that."

He snakes his arm around my waist as he rests his forehead against my arm.

There's a silence growing between us, but it's not a question mark, it's an ellipsis... We both know there's a connection. We both know what's going to happen next. And we're both hovering here in the remaining space between us, before the amazing idea of he and I becomes something real. The real thing will either be incredibly beautiful or beautifully terrible, but I am willing to let this man break my heart. It's a given that it will happen eventually. But at least I know that the journey to this heartbreak will feel good enough to make the pain worth it.

All those feelings I tucked away years ago for safe-keeping? I'm unlocking the chest, and it's up to Vince to decide if he can handle what's inside. But he's the first, and I secretly wish he could be the last man I ever open it up for.

How could I not?

*N*ina's fingers are combing through my hair, and I'm resting my face against her naked breast, tracing little circles around her belly with my fingertips. It's the calmest I've felt in years. I could spend the rest of the summer in this bed with this woman and not have any regrets. That's not true. I'm already starting to regret telling her she can go back to dating boring men in September.

"Hey?" She gives me a little pat on the shoulder.

"Yeah?"

"Should we go somewhere? Someplace in public where we can talk and get to know each other, without the potential for engaging in sexual activity?"

"That place doesn't exist in my world, darlin'."

"I mean, if you don't want to be seen in public with me..." Her voice trails off.

My head pops up. "What? Are you insane?"

"Well..."

I sit up and stare down at her. "Why wouldn't I want to be seen with you?"

"Because you're cool and I'm not."

"Oh right. Meet me by my locker at lunch and we'll walk to the cafeteria together. We can hang out by the brass doors after school, but my cool friends will probably ignore you."

"Yeah, I wish I hadn't said that out loud."

"If you're free on Saturday night, I'd like to take you to a party. My partner, Eve, is having a big birthday party. She's turning thirty-five. Should be a rager."

"Oh gosh. I don't know if I can handle a rager."

"Don't worry," I say, reaching around to grab her sweet ass. "I'll be the one doing the handling."

I get an arm punch for that.

"All night long, baby."

"I'd like that."

"Good. It's a date. Come on." I take her hand, lifting her up so we're face-to-face. "I wanna show you something."

She gives me a look, like...*again? Already?*

"It's not my dick, dirty bird. Get your mind out of the gutter and put your clothes on."

WATCHING NINA'S FACE AS SHE TAKES IN THE VIEW from my building's roof terrace is almost as fulfilling as watching her take in the view of my body. You can't fake that kind of appreciation. I don't think. I'm so glad the hipsters aren't up here tonight—it's just us and the café string lights and the moon and the stars and the Brooklyn Bridge and the Manhattan skyline. And the street noise and the voices of people shouting from the building across from me.

"Wow."

"Not bad, huh? I never get tired of it."

"So this is what people do, huh? Ride their motorcycles around Brooklyn, have sex in their awesome lofts, and then come up to their roof decks to enjoy the view?"

I grin and pull her to me, stand behind her with my arms wrapped around her waist. "*We* do. Sometimes." I kiss her neck. "Other times we'll stroll around Cobble Hill and go to the flea market and then have sex in my loft."

"I'd like that. What about other times?"

"Other times we'll take a drive out to Connecticut and then have sex in the back seat of my car like teenagers."

"You like Connecticut?"

"I like driving. And I'd like to have sex in the back seat of my car with you like teenagers."

"That's a lot of sex."

"You're a lot of sexy."

She giggles, lowering her head and shaking it. She really has no idea how hot she is. I've met exactly zero other girls like that around here.

"Have you lived in New York all your life?"

"Changing the subject, huh? I've lived in Brooklyn my whole life."

"Really?"

"Does that surprise you?"

"No, I guess not. But most people I know here moved from somewhere else."

"That doesn't surprise me. If I didn't grow up in Brooklyn, I'd probably move here too. Did you like living in Indiana?"

"I love Bloomington."

"Yeah?"

"Yeah. It's the perfect-sized town, I think."

"Why'd you move?"

She sighs, shrugging her shoulders. "When you've been in love in a small town and the person you thought you'd be with there for the rest of your life leaves without you, it's pretty hard to see every place you ever went to with him every single day. I stuck it out for a couple of years because I was too depressed to go anywhere else, but...I needed a change of scenery."

"Well you got one."

"I sure did."

I hate that some kid got to love this girl and then broke her heart so many years before I met her. I don't know what I'll have to say or do to get her to feel whatever it is she felt back then when she wasn't afraid of this kind of thing. But this summer I'm going to try everything. Even when it scares me.

I guess I was feeling insecure about the fact that she's been in love before and I haven't. But there are a lot of things that I've done that she hasn't, so maybe that balances the scales somehow. I don't know for sure what falling in love feels like. I just know that I'm starting to feel like the center of my universe is shifting in a way that it hasn't before. With someone who isn't family, anyway.

I ask her why she decided to move to Brooklyn, and

I know the answer as soon as she blushes and covers her mouth, shaking her head as she laughs.

"It's silly," she mutters.

"Tell me."

"Because of the HBO show *Girls*."

So many young women have moved here because of that show. I'm not complaining. It's not what I would have guessed for Nina, but it's not disappointing either. Usually these girls live in Williamsburg or Greenpoint and work at some hipster coffee place. That she ended up in Carroll Gardens teaching first grade and dating an older principal while wondering what it would be like to be Lena Dunham just makes her uniquely adorable and awesome.

THERE'S SOMETHING ABOUT THIS WOMAN THAT MAKES me feel like a boy who needs to dance around to impress her and like a man who wants to take care of her, at the same time. If I told Dr. Glass this, she'd probably shit herself. Not because it's a good way to feel but because it's too soon for this feeling to be real. She'd just tell me to wait until I'm really ready.

Fuck that.

What's wrong with now?

Now is all we have.

Shouldn't that be the big lesson when you lose someone you love?

Maybe I've already waited twenty-eight years for this.

I can't say that I was looking for it, and maybe I was

trying to avoid it, but I know I've found something in Nina.

My shrink might not approve, but ultimately, she's supposed to help me feel good. And I do. She's supposed to help me build the life that I want. And I'm doing that right now.

I know what lust feels like. There's something here on top of that. Or beneath it, or entwined with it. It's not about closing a deal with this woman. It's about opening things up and making something big and beautiful.

Speaking of making something big and beautiful— she turns me around so that I'm leaning back against the railing. And then she's pressed up against my chest, looking past me at the view, while her hand slowly reaches down the front of my sweatpants.

I remember the first time I viewed the loft and came up to this roof deck, saw the view, and it took my breath away and I instantly knew:

Mine. I have to have this.

But that was nothing compared to the view of Nina's sweet face as she's gently stroking me and the feeling I have of wanting this.

Mine.

Chapter Fourteen

VINCE

*A*s if I needed another sign that life as I know it has changed forever, the moment that really crystallizes things for me is when I'm on the F train, on my way home from a dinner meeting before picking Nina up for the party. The guy next to me is listening to his music so loud that I can hear every word of a-ha's "Take On Me" from his earbuds. And I keep thinking *That's exactly how I feel. That's how I've been feeling about Nina.*

Except the "I'll be gone" part. But the other stuff—at least the lines I can understand. It really *is* no better to be safe than sorry. But I do want her to feel safe with me. I don't want her to be sorry she kept seeing me. We keep talking away and she keeps shying away, but I'll be coming for her anyway and I'm slowly learning that life is okay.

Fuck me.

This is pathetic.

If my brother knew what was going on in my head

right now, he'd sucker-punch those pretty boy Norwegian eighties synth-pop thoughts right out of me. Or maybe one look at Nina and he'll wonder why it took me more than two seconds to decide to pursue her.

I keep thinking about how Mom would have loved her. And the fact that she uses the same dish soap and listens to Joni Mitchell. I'm not saying this is something Freudian or anything. It's just a coincidence. Or a sign. I'm pretty sure I'm not trying to make too big a deal out of it, but it's definitely doing something to my head. It makes me confused about how long I've known Nina. Time feels more elastic.

Or maybe I shouldn't have had two glasses of Scotch with dinner.

WHEN OUR MOUTHS AND TONGUES FINALLY PULL apart, she licks her lips and says, "Mmmm. Scotch?"

"Very good." I've been giving Nina a crash course in alcohol identification, mostly based on whatever taste is lingering on my tongue. Not that I drink all that often. So far, I've had her try shots of tequila, vodka, and whiskey at my place. And I mixed her up an Orgasm Cocktail after we finally came down from my roof deck. That was a great fucking night. I had Scotch after dinner last night too, before meeting up with her. She's a fast learner.

"Am I dressed okay for the party?" she asks, as if that's even a valid question. "My friend Marnie made me wear this."

"Your friend Marnie is a genius." She's wearing tight

jeans, spiky heels, a loose shimmery silver tank top, and hoop earrings. She's got on eyeliner or something tonight. It changes her face. Makes her look like a supermodel, but the kind you'd actually want to talk to. "Darlin', you are dressed more than okay. As long as you're okay with my hand up that top all night. You look stunning."

"I just wasn't sure if—I mean, I'll be meeting your family and co-workers, right? I don't want to look too..."

"Hot? You literally couldn't look less hot if you tried."

She furrows her brow at me.

"Wait. That came out wrong. You couldn't look *more* hot if you tried. You *always* look hot—there."

"Exactly how much Scotch did you have today?"

"I'm just drunk on your beauty, baby."

I hold the door to the Uber car open and get back in with her. I can see the driver's eyes bulge out of their sockets when he checks her out.

"Eyes on the road, buddy," I say as he pulls away from the curb in front of her building.

"Hi, how are you?" she says to the driver. Because she's friendly.

"Hey, how's it going," the driver replies. I can tell he's trying so hard to *not* sound flirtatious. And it pisses me off.

I lay another long kiss on Nina until she has to pull away to catch her breath. She clears her throat and looks out the window, smiling. I put my hand on her thigh, and I'm not going to let go of her all night.

I start laughing all of a sudden—remembering that she actually thought I was too cool to be seen in public with her. She looks back over at me quizzically. I can tell she thinks I'm drunk, but it really is just her effect on me. She might be too hot for me to be able to handle navigating her *and* the public at the same time. That has never been an issue for me before now.

I've dated nothing but hot women, but I've never felt so protective of one before. With Sadie it was because I was giving up my freedom to be with her, so I didn't want anyone else touching her or ogling her. With Nina, I just want her for myself. I've seen the nightlife. I've been a part of it since high school. I know what's up out there. I want to stay in and listen to her talk about chapter books and watch her face while I make her come. I'm not ready to share her yet. But I'll have to.

The cocktail bar that Eve and I chose for her birthday party is a cool place in Williamsburg, with a big private room. Eve doesn't know it yet, but my dad and brother and I are paying for everything tonight.

I lead Nina through the candle and Edison bulb–lit front room lounge, toward the back. I don't know the bartender who's working tonight, but I give him a nod. I see him checking out my girl. Can't blame him, but I give him a warning look. *Fucking bartenders.* I should know.

"I like the vibe here," she says. Like it's the first time she's ever said the word "vibe" in her life.

"Yeah, I know the guy who owns this place. We found another location for him in Red Hook. He's doing a whiskey bar over there."

"What should I drink tonight?" she asks, her face lighting up. "Wanna know what kind of mood I'm in?"

I stop and turn to face her. "I know exactly what I'm gonna make you—to put you in the mood I *want* you in."

"If it's another Orgasm, you'll have to work up to that."

"Hey, do I look like an amateur? First, I make you a French Kiss—but only if they have lavender bitters here, which they might not. Then you get a Hanky Panky, and then you get your Orgasm."

"Why, Mr. Devlin. I will remind you that I am a lightweight. You'd better choose *one* and choose wisely."

"I *have* chosen one," I say, kissing her on the cheek. For the first time ever, I'm confident that I've chosen wisely. I put my arm around her shoulder and open the door to the back room.

The amber up-lighting, chandeliers, exposed brick walls, leather seating, and deep red velvet curtains create a cozy, sexy vibe. But right now the room is packed and warm and thumping. I didn't realize we were so late to the party. The DJ is playing 50 Cent's "In Da Club," and everyone in here is going nuts. The whole room is a dance floor. I can see Eve in the middle of the room, dancing with her wife and pointing to herself, yelling "It's my birthday!"

Even our uptight lawyer is shaking his arms and attempting a heel-toe step. I guide Nina through the crowd a few feet and then turn to face her. My hands slide down to her hips. I position my leg between hers and try to ignore how surprised she seems to be that I'm actually dancing. Like what—does she think I'm too cool to dance? I grab her ass and pull her as close as possible to me, my thigh right up in there between her legs. In that place where I could live for days. It only takes a second for her hips to start swaying back and forth, her arms up in the air, head nodding to the beat like everyone else in here.

She moves her shoulders and ribs in a way that is very impressive, and I can't stop from sliding my hands up under her tank top. I did warn her this would happen. She smirks—so hot—puts her hands over mine, and slides them back down to her ass. I'll take it. I'll take all of it. I kiss her, and within seconds, we're making out so hot and heavy. We're pressed up against each other, and everyone else is so into doing their own thing, I don't even care that my whole sales team is in here somewhere.

She finally pulls away from me and runs her hands through her hair while mouthing the words to the song at me—*twist!* I guess the youngsters in Bloomington listen to hip-hop too.

Out of the corner of my eye, I can see Eve making her way over to us, holding her giant margarita glass up over people's heads. She's staring at Nina with her face all scrunched up like she's scrutinizing her. "Go shorty," I yell out along with the song, "it's your birthday!" But she stops right next to Nina and yells out: "*Miss Parks?*"

Nina freezes, stares at Eve. Her eyes widen and she says, "Tyler's mom! Hi!"

"Oh my God! Hi!" Eve looks at me, pointing crazily between herself and Nina. "We know each other! She taught my son last year! Holy fuck!" She slaps my shoulder. "*Hah!*"

Nina has slowly let go of me and stepped back, straightening up her clothes.

Eve takes a huge slug of her margarita and then almost spits it out and yells out at Nina, "I don't usually drink like this—I swear!"

"I don't usually dance like this—I swear!"

"Oh my God, I almost didn't recognize you with the makeup and the earrings and the Vince—but oh my God! It's Miss Parks!"

"Happy birthday! You must be having so much fun!" Nina shouts, trying to change the subject.

I should be more surprised that my business partner already knows Nina, but my brain is too busy picturing "Miss Parks" in a buttoned-down blouse, tight skirt, and spiky heels, holding up a ruler and telling me to stay after school because I've been a very bad boy.

I have to physically shake my head to rid myself of that image.

I can't believe it didn't occur to me that Eve would actually know Nina. Eve hardly ever brings her son around to the office or talks about him because she's always talking about "separation of church and state." I think she just doesn't want all us guys thinking of her as a mom first and foremost. As if we thought of her as anything other than a kickass broker who's a cool lesbian with a hot wife.

But it makes me strangely happy to know that Eve and Nina knew each other before Nina knew me. It's another social connection beyond our lying, cheating exes.

It may take a while for Nina to see this as a strangely happy connection, though. I can tell she's horrified that one of her student's parents has seen us grinding away on each other.

Eve yells out that she'll talk to us later and wades through the crowd to talk to one of our clients. I look around, not seeing my dad or Gabe. I yell into Nina's ear, "You want that drink now?"

She just shrugs her shoulders. "I guess?" She shakes her head and covers her face.

"Hey. What?"

"It's Tyler's mom!"

"It's awesome!"

She shakes her head. "It's humiliating."

"Why?"

"I don't know."

"Come here." I pull her back out the doors to the front room, where it's not as loud. "Have you never run into someone from your school when you were out in public before?"

"Not while I had my tongue down a guy's throat and was rubbing up on him!"

Oh my God, you are so cute. "We were dancing! Everyone's dancing. You think I haven't seen Eve with her tongue halfway down her wife's throat?"

She paces around, shaking her hands like they're wet. "That's not the same thing."

"Are you embarrassed to be seen with *me*?"

"No! God, no. This is just so different from how I usually am."

"Hey." I put my hands on either side of her face. "You're not in class right now. It's your summer break. It's not like you're shooting a porno. Or heroin. You're allowed to be a complex adult human being. Just because you teach little kids that doesn't mean you have to live like one your whole life."

She looks up at me like I just said something brilliant. When she kisses me, I do feel brilliant. I feel everything.

"Okay," she agrees with a nod. "Is your family here?"

"I didn't see them, but it's possible."

"Well, maybe don't hump my leg while they're around."

"I make no promises. And I'm pretty sure *you* were humping *my* leg."

Her hand goes to her face when she laughs like a girl, and God I love it when she does that.

I open the door to the back room again. Thankfully the song that's now playing is some cheesy Beyoncé ballad that we don't have to dance to—and you could not pay me enough to dance to this song. Ever.

"Oh, I love this song!" she exclaims, turning to me. Her eyes are all lit up. "Can we slow-dance to this?!"

"Okay!"

Fuck.

I am in so much trouble.

Chapter Fifteen

NINA

"So, you're the reason he's been smiling lately." Tyler's mom appears next to me as I stand by the bar, waiting for Vince to return from the restroom. Her curly hair looks adorably insane, and she looks like a very happy birthday girl.

"Oh, I don't know. Why—does he not usually?"

"Hah! Mr. Seriously Sexy? I don't think so." She smacks my arm with the back of her hand. "I can't believe it's you!"

"How's Tyler?"

"He's great! He's with his sperm donor dad for the week. He really loved you as a teacher," she gushes with her hand to her heart. "You completely opened him up. Where's that wife of mine? I told her you were here—she flipped out. We're always talking about how you turned things around for Ty."

"I appreciate you saying that, but he probably would have started to open up anyway as he got older."

"No. It was you. Let's hope you can work the same

magic on our boy Vince. Turn his life around. Wouldn't that be nice."

I smile. "Actually, I think it's safe to say that he's the one who's turning my life around."

"I'm sure, but still." She waves her hand. "Thank God Sadie's gone. Blech. He was always in such a bad mood when he was with her those last few months." She shudders.

Someone comes up behind Eve and hugs her. She looks back to see who it is and screams, thus ending our conversation. I wish we could have talked longer. I would have liked to hear more about how miserable Vince was with Sadie.

I hear Vince call my name, and I turn to see him standing with two other men and a lady. They are all staring at me when Vince waves me over.

The older man looks like a heavyset present-day Alec Baldwin, and the younger man looks like a bigger, more angular version of Vince. The middle-aged woman standing in between them looks unequivocally thrilled to be near them, and I can see why. The Devlins all have the cool-sexy-handsome gene. God help us.

The woman waves at me, holding out her hand. "I'm Sharon! It's nice to meet you!"

"This is my dad's girlfriend," Vince says, and Sharon starts beaming like he just proclaimed her the queen of the universe.

I shake her hand. "Hi, I'm Nina. It's very nice to meet you."

"This is my dad, Neil Devlin."

Neil Devlin has a poker face and mischievous dark

eyes. He looks down at me as he shakes my hand, saying nothing.

"How do you do."

He bows his head and slow-blinks his eyes, watching me. I can't tell if he hates me or not.

The bigger, bolder version of Vince, who has been studying me while standing very still and holding a tumbler, takes my hand. He doesn't really shake it, doesn't let go of it either. "You really dating this idiot?"

"My brother, Gabe." Vince is shaking his head, amused.

"Hi, Gabe. Yes, I really am."

"Well, you ever want to hang with a real man...you come see me."

"And then he'll send you to the *real* man in the family—me. And I'll send you back to Vince."

"And I will keep you the hell away from these assholes from now on."

Sharon giggles as Neil puts his arm around her.

"The new nanny watching Charlie tonight?" Vince asks his father.

"Yeah. Karen." He looks at me. "We hire a sixty-year-old nanny this time, and this guy can't even remember her name."

Good to know.

"I remember her name," Vince protests. "It's Karen. Karen Walters."

"Karen Williams," says Gabe.

"It's Karen Winters," Sharon tells them.

"See why I keep her around," Neil Devlin says, giving Sharon a squeeze. I get a wink from him. "We're very happy to meet you, Nina. Vince has been slightly more tolerable since he met you, which is saying a lot."

"Actually, he's even less tolerable because he just spaces out and smiles like a moron in meetings." Gabe punches Vince's arm.

These guys are so cute. It's too much.

"Okay, let's go get you that drink now." Vince pulls me back toward the bar, and I wave to the Devlins and Sharon. "That was terrible," he says, head lowered.

"Awww, come on," I say, rubbing his back. "Haven't you ever run into your family when you were out in public before? Are you embarrassed to be seen with *me*?"

"Okay, smartass. You ready for your French Kiss?"

"Am I ever."

He goes behind the bar, salutes the bartender with two fingers, and starts inspecting the stock.

In no time, a clean-cut man in a polo shirt is standing right next to me as I lean against the counter. He looks over and nods at me. I smile politely.

"I'm Mark," he says, holding out his hand to me.

"Hi, Mark. I'm Nina." He may be a co-worker or client of Vince's, so I don't make a point of moving away from him.

"You having a good night, Nina?"

"So far so good. You?"

"Getting better. Can I get you a drink?"

"I got her covered, man." Vince's voice is deeper than usual.

Mark raises his eyebrow at him. "Hey, can I get a gin and tonic?"

I guess they *don't* know each other.

"Yeah, you should definitely walk your loafers on over there and ask the bartender for one of those."

"Excuse me?"

"I think you heard me." Vince's jaw is so rigid as he leans against the counter, flexing his muscles.

I force a laugh. "Um, he's not the bartender. He's just making me a drink."

"I think you'd be better off getting a drink with *me*, somewhere else," Mark says.

"Are you fucking kidding me?" Vince slams down the bottle he was holding and starts out around the bar.

I maneuver myself to block this from Vince, pulling Vince, with all my might, away and out of the room.

"I wasn't gonna hit him," he assures me unconvincingly.

"I'd just like to talk to you outside please."

I lead him through the lounge and toward the front doors without looking back at him.

I can control a room full of six-year-olds. I should be able to get one twenty-eight-year-old man to behave himself. *Here's how it is. Here are the rules.* Rules bind our anxiety so we don't have to worry about what we *should* be doing. I learned that while I was getting my degree. And while I was dating Russell.

I let go of his hand when we're on the sidewalk. No one else is around. I put my hands on my hips. Vince looks defiant but also a tiny bit ashamed.

"You can't talk to people like that. Isn't everyone a potential client for you?"

"We have a strict No Douchebag client policy."

"Well, it makes me uncomfortable when you talk to someone like that just because he was talking to me."

"Sorry. I didn't realize you were so into him."

"Vince. I was not *into* him. I'm here with you. I'm not going to ignore men who talk to me, especially when I have no idea if they know you or not, but I have no interest in getting to know them. You can trust me."

"I do trust you. It's that guy I don't trust."

"Well, I can't make you trust someone. But please try not to let your feathers get ruffled. This is our first time out on a real date, so I'd prefer it if there were no bloodshed."

He looks at me like I've been speaking a foreign language, and then a smile spreads across his face and he lowers his head, laughing. "'Try not to let your feathers get ruffled?' What are you—ninety?"

"Well, now you're just trying to ruffle *my* feathers," I say, putting up my dukes.

He grabs my hands and pulls my arms around his waist. "Baby, I want to ruffle your feathers until you're too exhausted to fly away."

"Yeah?"

"Hell yeah."

"Is there anyone else whose feathers you want to ruffle anytime soon?"

"Hell no."

"Well, we're on the same page, then. You asked me to give you the summer. How about we officially agree that we will only be with each other this summer? To eliminate anxiety."

His face gets so serious, and I almost regret my

approach. "What if I still want you when the summer's over?"

It's difficult to get your facial muscles to form a smile when you're completely melting on the sidewalk, but somehow I manage. "We can revisit this issue in September."

"Plan on it. Deal." He cradles my hand in his face and kisses my mouth. "I'm all yours this summer."

"I'm all yours this summer."

Even under the dim streetlight, I can see that his eyes are sparkling. "You are something else."

"Thanks?"

"Thank *you*. I hope you don't have plans for tomorrow morning, 'cuz I'm gonna take you to brunch."

"*Really? I love* brunch."

"I had a feeling."

"Shall we return to the party now?"

He cranes his neck, looks around over my shoulder. "There's an alley over there. I could ruffle your feathers a little more first."

I spank his perfect butt. "Back to the party, sir. That will have to wait until we're back at your place."

He groans and takes my hand as we head back to the front door of the bar. "You're mean, Miss Parks."

"It's for your own good," I say and then lean in to whisper in his ear: "Trust me, you're going to want to see me in the bonkers lingerie I have in my purse." Words I have certainly never uttered before in my life.

I hold up my tiny purse, and he stops in his tracks, pulls out his phone, and opens up his Uber app. I take his phone away from him. "No—we have to say good-bye to everyone first."

"You are slowly killing me, Miss Parks."

As we make our way through the front of the bar, I notice a young woman watching us. Vince doesn't see her. In one second, her facial expression reveals so many things when she watches Vince—lust, hope, anger, bitterness, wistfulness. I know in the pit of my stomach that she has probably slept with him, and because she doesn't approach him, he probably hasn't seen her since.

Finally, after he has passed by her, she calls out, "Vince."

He looks back at her, still holding my hand, and I see no hint in his face that seeing her causes him to feel any emotions at all. "Oh hey, good to see you. Have a good night." Polite, pleasant, and not at all personal. He puts his arm around me, and we retreat into the private room. I don't look back to see the woman's reaction, but I know how I would feel if I were in her shoes. I try not to think about whether or not I will be in her shoes —or when. For now, I believe him when he tells me he's mine. All I have to do is get through the summer without losing my mind. I've already lost my heart.

Chapter Sixteen

NINA

*A*lmost overnight, I suddenly have the kind of summer schedule that I'd dreamed of having before I moved to Brooklyn and got caught up in Russell's regimented weekends of foodie adventures, jazz concerts, and antiquing.

I finally saw *Hamilton* on Broadway. Who lives in New York for three years without managing to see *Hamilton*? It was just as electrifying as meeting Vince, and I left both of them feeling young and super-charged and ready for anything.

When I was with Russell, I must have given off a *Don't look at me/don't talk to me vibe*, because I swear—men never used to check me out when I walked around town. They never used to strike up conversations with me in line at the market. Ironically, now is when I'm totally uninterested in getting to know another man, but I feel so open. And it's all because of Vince Devlin.

This is, without a doubt, the best summer I have had since moving to Brooklyn. It's the best summer of my life, if I'm being honest. I almost don't even think about what it will be like once school starts up again. When I'll be asleep by ten p.m., using faux swear words again, and seeing my fucking ex-fiancé five days a week. For now, I am more awake and busier than ever. Ignoring every lingering ghost thought of Russell and Sadie while staying focused on Vince. He has shown me so much of Brooklyn, usually on the fly in the middle of the day, between his meetings—when I'm not hanging out with Marnie or my other teacher friends.

He'll just call me up and say: "You like to doodle, right? You been to the Brooklyn Art Library? I'll meet you there in a half hour." And then we'll spend an hour looking through an amazing collection of artists' sketchbooks. When we're walking to get ice cream in Greenpoint, he's like: "Hey, you like cats?" and we take a little detour to see the Cat Village—a colony of feral cats that keep the local rodent population in check. At night, I'll get a call after his last meeting: "Hey, you feel like going out to hear some music? A buddy of mine's performing tonight." And then he'll take me to the Brooklyn Academy of Music to see his buddy perform.

Anything can happen when I'm with him, and so far there have been no more incidents when other men are friendly to me. Like the Italian waiter at this cozy neighborhood joint where we're getting lunch in the back garden. Vince even seems amused by the ostentatious way this fellow is flirting with me. After we order, I pull out a book from my bag and place it on the table in front of him.

"What's this?"

"Just a little gift. I was browsing the bookstore this

morning, and I wanted you to have a copy of this. It's one of my favorite poetry books."

He has such a big smile on his face as he picks it up. "Nobody's ever given me a book as a gift before. Not since I was a kid."

"Really?"

"Yeah. Thank you. I will read every word. I have something for you too, actually. In the trunk of my car. Which is at my dad's place. I'll give it to you tonight. Who's Rumi?"

"Rumi was a thirteenth century mystic poet and is one of the most popular poets in America, actually. He wrote so beautifully about love and longing and opening your heart to all of life's experiences. Even the painful ones. It got me through a lot, back in Bloomington. It's just beautiful, and...when I read a lot of these now, they remind me of you." I can't look up at him to see his expression. I've laid out so much more on the table than just that book. I laugh. "Before you, my biggest form of rebellion was reading Rumi poems when my dad was teaching classes on Chaucer and Shakespeare's sonnets."

"You really still think you're rebelling by being with me?" He is amused more than offended, but it's definitely both.

"Well no, I mean...I just...I had never had a one-night stand with a stranger before."

"Uh-huh. Well, it doesn't really count as a one-night stand anymore now, does it?"

"No. And I'm glad. But you were still a stranger."

"Everyone's a stranger at first, Nina."

Another excellent point.

"Were you on the debate team in high school, by any chance?"

"No, but I did go to third base with one of the girls on the debate team. After giving a very compelling argument about why she should let me."

I burst out laughing.

He grabs my hand and kisses the back of it. "I love that you gave me this. Thank you." He puts it in his leather messenger bag and then reaches for my hand again. "Listen, I can't go out tonight, but—"

"That's fine," I blurt out a little too quickly, trying to hide my disappointment.

"But...maybe you'd like to join us for dinner at my dad's place. They've been bugging me about wanting to see you again. It's Taco Tuesday at Casa Devlin. Unless my dad forgets to buy the ingredients again, and then it's Tater Tot Tuesday. Plus, like, one vegetable maybe."

"I'd love that. Yes. That sounds like fun."

"Oh yeah. It's like a *Fast and Furious* movie but with mediocre tacos and no cars. We can pick up Charlie at his day camp here in Carroll Gardens and then head over to Cobble Hill. His nanny gets off early today."

"Oh, I get to meet Charlie?" This feels significant. Charlie seems like such an important person in Vince's life, and I could tell he was waiting before talking about him more or introducing me to him. Probably because of the nanny-banging thing too.

"Yeah. It's time you met the little turd."

"Is he at the day camp on Smith Street?"

"Yeah, you know it?"

"Of course! It's a great program. Some of my friends

teach at summer day camps. I was considering it for this year."

"Well, I'm glad you're free to hang with me."

"Yeah, that worked out pretty well." I consider for a moment before asking him another question. But now that the door has cracked open a little... "Can you tell me about Charlie's mother? So I don't say the wrong thing in front of your family."

"Well, she's out of the picture. Has been since she ran off with some millionaire Greek guy two years ago."

"Wow."

"Yeah. Clara. She and my dad never got married. But they were together for seven years, even though she was a piece of work from day one. She had a few good qualities, I mean, she wasn't all terrible. Except for the fact that she just up and left her six-year-old son with barely any explanation."

My heart aches for all of them. "I can't even imagine."

"It was bad. But you know. My dad and brother and I were already working together at the brokerage, so we just started working together more on taking care of Charlie. He's such a good kid. Breaks my heart. But he's pretty tough. He's definitely the smartest of all us Devlin guys."

Hearing Vince talk about his little brother like this is making my ovaries ache. I so want to ask him about his own mother, but it doesn't seem like the right time. He has pulled out his phone to check his texts and emails. We've accomplished enough for one lunch already.

Chapter Seventeen

NINA

From a block away, I know which boy is Charlie without Vince ever having to point him out to me. Dark hair, sweet magnetic face and energy, sad eyes. He's got his backpack slung over one little shoulder and a book in one hand while he looks around, kicking the sidewalk with the toe of his Chuck Taylors, pretending to ignore the kids around him who aren't talking to him. He spots us coming toward him and looks happy to see Vince but confused seeing him with me. He waits for us to reach him, studying me the way I've been studied by all of the Devlin males I've met so far.

Definitely a Ponyboy.

"Hey, buddy. You ready to go?" Vince lets go of my hand and goes over to the other side of Charlie so that we're flanking him as we continue down the sidewalk.

"Yeah."

"This is my friend Nina. Remember I told you about her?"

Charlie looks up at me, unsmiling. "Hey."

"Hi. It's nice to meet you, Charlie. You have a good day at camp?"

"It was all right."

"Nina's coming to have dinner with us tonight."

"Did Dad remember to get all the taco stuff?"

"I hope so. I sent him a text to remind him."

Charlie looks up at me while we walk and then looks over at his brother and asks with a sheepish grin, "So you're the girl Vince is boning now?"

I blurt out a laugh, but Vince looks horrified. "Hey! He learned that from Gabe, not me." He playfully smacks him on the back of his head. "We don't talk to women like that, kid."

I nod toward the book in his hand, changing the subject. "You're reading *Matilda*? I loved that book when I was your age."

He shrugs. "A girl gave it to me today. I haven't read it yet."

"Wow," I say, looking at Vince. "When a girl gives you *a book,* that means she really likes you." With one sentence, I manage to make both Devlins blush at the same time. It's a tiny victory.

Charlie growls and raises his fists up. "Grrrr! She's *not* my girlfriend!" He jumps around, having the kind of sudden spaz attack that I'm very used to from little boys. So much energy. "I. Don't. Like. Girls!" He suddenly takes off running like a maniac.

"*Oy!* No running—get back here!" Vince's voice is loud and dominant.

Charlie kicks his leg up in the air midrun while squealing, and I know before his feet hit the ground that he's going to land all wrong. He stumbles and wipes out, hands first, but he manages to hang on to the book —which tells me a lot.

"Shit," Vince says under his breath. I see the look of panic in his eyes, but he tries not to speed up his pace, to avoid panicking or embarrassing Charlie. Which is what I've learned to do.

When we reach him, Charlie is hunched over and trying very hard to look tough, but his hand and knuckles are scraped and bleeding and the rims around his eyes are red.

"You okay?" Vince kneels down to muss up his brother's hair. "You're okay, right? You little spaz. Can you get up?"

"Yeah."

"Actually, I think I might have something in my purse that'll clean up that scrape." I kneel down on the cement beside Charlie and open up my giant day bag, pulling out the container of oatmeal chocolate chip cookies I made this afternoon and placing it on the ground. "It's important to clean up these little scrapes as soon as possible. I know because I have to do it a lot."

"You fall down a lot?" Charlie's voice is constricted, but he's still teasing me.

"Nina's a first-grade teacher," explains Vince with a hint of pride in his voice.

"I am. So I'm around a lot of boys who wipe out, but it happens to *me* when I play kickball with them."

Charlie snort-laughs. I pull out around twenty baggies with different daily necessities in them—sugar-free gummy bears, makeup, sparkly gel colored pens, cotton balls, bandages. I find my little bottle of Bactine near the bottom of my purse.

"What else you got in there, Miss Parks?" Vince knows I've been keeping a slender cosmetics bag full of condoms in here lately.

"No bags of frozen peas, unfortunately."

As I clean up Charlie's hands with Bactine and he hisses because of the minor sting, I ask him, "What's the worst time you ever wiped out?"

"On my bike."

"Yeah?"

"Oooh, that was ugly," Vince says, wincing. "Right into a tree. Didn't break anything though. You were lucky."

"We were with Sadie," Charlie says wistfully.

Vince goes silent.

"Yeah?" I decide to side-step that comment. "The worst time I ever wiped out was on a bike too. When I was ten. I was going down a hill really fast, and the front wheel hit a big branch and I went flying."

"Whoa. Did you bleed?"

"Oh yeah. It wasn't that bad though. Had to get a few stitches. You ever had stitches?"

"No."

"You are lucky, then. Stitches is when a doctor sews up your skin so it grows back together."

I put the last bandage on Charlie's hand. "Gross! With a needle?"

"Yup. With a needle and this bright blue kind of thread."

"Can I see?"

"Nope—I don't have them anymore. See?" I hold up my palm to show him where the stitches were. "The thread they use just kind of disappears eventually. They melt into your skin or something."

"No way."

"Yeah way. You ready to get up?"

He nods and gets up, still holding his Roald Dahl book. I toss everything back into my bag.

"Can I have a cookie?"

"I don't know," I say, looking up at his big brother. "Can he?"

"Just one. But only if I can have one too."

I open the container, hand out two cookies, and then put the container back in my bag. Vince takes a bite before holding out his hand to help me up. "Mmmm! That's so good. Right, Charlie?"

"I like it."

"All the boys in your class must be so in love with you, Miss Parks," Vince whispers into my ear as I'm standing.

"I do get a lot of shiny apples on my desk."

"I'd give you a banana."

"And I'd make you sit in the corner all day until you learned some manners."

"I'd never learn any manners if it meant I got to stay in your corner all day."

"Why is your voice like that?" Charlie asks him. "You sound like a girl." It's not entirely true, but Vince does sound different.

Vince clears his throat. "I do not—punk." Now he sounds like The Rock.

Charlie and I laugh, but I feel like crying and I don't even know why.

———

IT IS DIFFICULT TO EAT WHEN YOU'RE SURROUNDED BY so much testosterone.

The tacos are, in fact, delicious. Mr. Devlin's townhouse is gorgeous. I'm not sure why I'm here tonight and Sharon isn't, but it's kind of great being entertained by these four boys. Gabe, Neil, and Charlie are having a grand old time telling embarrassing stories about Vince, and it's so cute.

"When Vinnie was thirteen..." Gabe says, pointing to his brother.

Vince swats at Gabe's extended finger and grumbles, "Don't call me Vinnie."

"I told Vinnie that the magic line for getting into girls' pants was *I've got so much love in me—I just want to put it in you*. And he said it to this girl after a dance. She busted a gut laughing, ran, and told everyone."

"She did not laugh."

"Well, she didn't let you put it in her either!"

"Because I didn't try to—we were thirteen. Shut up."

"Well, that line works on me every time, lemme tell ya. I am just *filled* with his love."

After a beat, during which I can hardly believe I said that out loud, Gabe, Neil, and Vince burst out laughing. Charlie laughs too, even though I really hope he doesn't actually get what we're talking about.

"Where'd you find this one again?" his dad asks him. "On stage at the Comedy Cellar?"

"Yep, she'll be there all week."

"No really, how did you guys meet?" Neil asks.

Ahh, he hasn't told him. Well, why would he?

"Just in the neighborhood," Vince says. "I saw her in a store and asked her for a date."

The PG version. Sounds good to me.

"And you actually said yes?" Gabe asks me, truly disbelieving.

"Eventually," I tell him coyly.

Vince squeezes my thigh under the table. The way he's looking at me right now, I actually do feel like I'm filled with his love, and it makes it even more difficult for me to digest my dinner. Seeing him with his family like this is making feel so stupidly emotional, and it's totally unexpected.

I wipe my fingers on the napkin and clear my throat. "I've had way too much lemonade. I need to be excused."

"There is seriously no excuse for you dating my brother when you could have me," Gabe quips.

"Down that hall, first door on your left, hon." Neil gives me a little wink.

"Thanks."

I squeeze Vince's hand as I get up. His concerned face is forcing me to look away from him, or I'll just start crying at the table like a freak.

As soon as the bathroom door clicks shut, tears just start squirting out of my eyeballs. *What is happening to me?* I grab two Kleenexes and press them up against the inner corners of my eyes. Thank God I'm not wearing eye makeup today.

It's been so much easier for me to throw myself into this rebound-summer fling thing by categorizing Vince as the kind of guy I could never really have a long-term relationship with. But right now that's what I want, and it's just crazy.

Pull it together, Parks!

You are the boss of you—not your hormones.

If you can't just enjoy this and have fun in the moment, then you don't even deserve to get boned by a hot guy for two months.

He knocks quietly on the door. "You okay in there?"

I let out an involuntary sigh. "I'm great! One second!" I blow my nose, flush the Kleenex down the toilet to get rid of the evidence, and then splash cold water on my eyes, dabbing at them with a hand towel.

"You can do this," I say to my reflection before unlocking the door.

Before I can step out into the hallway, Vince guides me back inside the bathroom and shuts the door. He hugs me and kisses my neck.

"Hi."

"Hi."

"Sorry if those assholes are being a little too intense."

"Oh my God, no—your family is wonderful."

"Are you upset that I didn't tell them about how we know each other?"

"No. God no. I get it. That's basically what I told my parents too."

"Okay. Because honestly, I barely even remember

how we met. It feels like we've known each other forever." He pulls away from the hug and says, "Okay that was literally the cheesiest thing I've ever said. I just threw up in my mouth a little. I don't even blame you if that grosses you out."

I grab his face and kiss him so hard, neither of us can breathe.

If it's a mistake to fall for him like this, then it's the best *fucking* mistake I have ever made.

AFTER DINNER, VINCE DROVE ME HOME AND GAVE ME my gift: two record albums (Joni Mitchell's *Blue* and *Court and Spark*) and a beautiful vintage record player. He said it was making him nuts that I just listened to Spotify on my phone.

He went back to his dad's place to stay with Charlie while Neil spent the night at Sharon's, and I listened to "Help Me" and "A Case of You" over and over until I fell asleep.

THIS MORNING I WOKE UP TO A CALL FROM HIM, asking me if I wanted to meet him in an hour at the Transit Garden, which is not far from where I live. It's a private community garden that I've always been curious about, and it turns out the Devlins are members and they have a memorial planter there in honor of Colette Devlin.

He said he was going to stop by there to water the plants on the way to a meeting.

I managed to tell him I'd join him without getting all choked up on the phone.

I had been so relentlessly unemotional for years, as some kind of defense mechanism. Now that Vince has unlocked something in me, I feel like an actress who's losing her Schmidt while giving her Oscar acceptance speech: *I have so many things to be thankful for! Thank you to the Academy of Hot Guy Arts and Sciences. For Vince Devlin's penis. His mouth and hands and tongue. Thank you for his eyes and voice and the way he smells. For all the exciting places he's been taking me—in New York and inside my own heart and mind. For giving me this opportunity to experience love in this new way. Also, I'd like to thank whoever invented multiple orgasms, because* wow. *My skin is amazing right now.*

It just feels like such a significant thing for him to invite me to...but it may be no different from all the other things he's called me up to ask me to meet him for.

Regardless, I show up with a small lavender plant that I got at my favorite garden center in Boerum Hill. When I tell him that I was hoping there'd be room for it in their planter, he makes a little guttural noise before saying, "Thanks, that's sweet. She loved lavender." He inhales the plant. "Yeah, she loved this stuff." His eyes are pink-rimmed. I'm a jerk for loving that, but I've made him blush and get teary-eyed within twenty-four hours—I don't want to push it.

The garden is lovely. Surrounded by a brick wall and metal fence, it's a rustic little private oasis in the middle of Carroll Gardens. Vince is dressed for work, so I offer to do the planting and watering. They have a raised planter box with sunflowers and geraniums and marigolds.

As I'm tucking the plant into the soil, something occurs to me. "She's not actually...*in* here, right? Her ashes?"

"No. She's buried at Green-Wood. She just loved plants, so we got this for her."

I wait for him to offer more information.

Finally, after a lengthy silence, all he says is, "She had cancer. For like a year. It sucked. It seemed like she was getting better, but then all of a sudden, she just..."

"Oh, Vince." I wipe my dirty hand on my jeans before reaching out to touch his arm. "I'm so sorry."

"I had a hard time dealing with it. But she was just the best." He looks at me as though he's going to say something else. But he doesn't. He suddenly retreats into some place that I'm not a part of, and I let him go there on his own. I spend more time dusting dirt off leaves than I need to, until he finally mutters, "You want to come with me to grab a coffee on my way? I gotta be someplace in twenty."

We hold hands on the way to the coffee place, even though he talks on the phone to Eve about some deal they're closing for most of the way.

"You got big plans for today?" he asks, opening the door and not looking at me.

"I'm meeting Marnie for lunch, and then I'm going to catch up on a bunch of professional guides and education blogs and start planning next year's curriculum."

"Really? But it's still the middle of summer."

"It's never too soon to prepare for the next term."

"Geez. Just show the kids a bunch of videos the first week of classes, Miss Parks. That's all they want anyway."

I notice a woman staring at us, sitting at a corner table by herself. I get the same shiver of awareness that I had at the bar, the night of Eve's party. This is another one of his exes. He doesn't see her, and she looks less interested in talking to him than the other one did. I manage to ignore her, but when Vince's coffee is ready before my chai tea latte is, he kisses me and has to leave before I do, to get to his appointment.

"I'll call you later, okay? I might be able to cancel my dinner if you're free."

"Sure. Have a good day."

I watch him walk out of the coffee shop, pretty sure he's completely unaware of the girl in the corner.

"You should be careful." The sultry voice comes from right behind me. She says it so casually, as if we're friends in midconversation. I turn to face her. Though just as striking, she has a very different look from the other woman. A tiny diamond stud in her nose and great shag haircut makes me think she is some kind of musician, although I can't help but wonder if this is Sadie. She arranges her messenger bag strap on her shoulder.

I clear my throat. "Hi. Do I know you?"

She smiles and shakes her head as she puts on her aviator sunglasses. "No, but I know exactly how you're feeling right now. He take you for a ride on his bike yet?"

I blink.

"Yeah. Don't let those sad eyes fool you. He's hot.

And he can seem like the nicest guy in the world some-times, but he'll ghost you sooner or later. He always disappears. Enjoy it while it lasts." She shrugs, as if what she's just said is no big deal. "That's just him. That's just how it goes."

And then she disappears out the door, leaving me to my warm chai tea latte and stunned icy silence.

Chapter Eighteen

VINCE

*A*fter I had taken Nina home from dinner at my dad's, I got a text from my dad that said: ***For fuck sake she's great. Please don't fuck things up with this one.***

Nice vote of confidence for her, not so much for me.

From my brother: ***She is literally perfect. If you don't marry her, I will. Fuck you.***

That's a first from Gabe, who hasn't dated anyone for longer than two months in his entire horndog life.

Eve hasn't shut up about Nina since her birthday party.

Charlie's already asking when she's coming over again. That doesn't surprise me. She was so great with him, especially when he fell down. Seeing her with all those baggies full of mom purse stuff spread out over the sidewalk, I had this weird urge to impregnate her. *That* was a first for me.

I probably shouldn't have taken her to the garden so soon after dinner with my family. I've felt a little off since then, but it's definitely not Nina's fault. Nothing's Nina's fault. She is perfect. For the first time in my life, I'm wondering if I'm good enough for someone. I've never wanted such a good woman before. I've never wanted so badly for a good woman to want me. It one hundred percent blows. But I still need to be with her all the time.

I know I'm moving too fast, but I don't know how else to move. Especially when it comes to her. What we have is still so new, and there are still things she doesn't know about me. But I'm starting to feel like I could lose her any day now. I thought I could win her over in a summer, but each day that passes just feels like a death march toward September. It's how I always felt about going back to school, only this is so much more than losing my freedom when school starts. I could lose Nina. She'll realize how different we are, and our schedules won't mesh. She'll be seeing that fucking principal every day, and she'll remember this is just a rebound.

Fuck. This is why Dr. Glass wanted me to keep up with the sessions and wait to start things up with Nina. All these fucking feelings that used to stay buried, back when I'd fuck and run.

Whatever. I still have another month to get my shit together. A lot can happen in a month.

SHE DOESN'T ANSWER UNTIL THE THIRD RING, WHICH is weird.

"Hi," she says, her voice soft.

"Did I wake you up or something?"

"No. Not at all."

"You sure?"

"Yes." She clears her throat. "Hi."

"Hi. Listen, I really hate to bother you with this, but Charlie's at day camp and his new part-time nanny has some family emergency all of a sudden. She can't pick him up. Are you busy? I know you said you have work to do, so you can say no. I can try someone else."

"I can get him," she says without hesitation. "Of course. Do you want me to take him somewhere or bring him back to my place?"

"Thank you so much. Yeah, take him to your place. I'll pick you guys up after work, and then we'll drop him off at Gabe's and you and I can go to dinner."

"Uh-huh."

"You still want to go to dinner?"

"Yeah, of course. Listen, don't hesitate to call me if you need someone to pick Charlie up or drop him off at the day camp. It's so close to me, it's no trouble."

I feel my jaw tensing up. I don't want to turn her into another nanny here. She's just being sweet, I know. "Okay, yeah, thanks. Hopefully it won't be necessary."

Silence on the other end.

"Sooo, text me when you've got Charlie and I'll call when I'm leaving the office, yeah?"

"Yeah."

"Okay, thanks again. Bye."

"Bye."

What the fuck was that? Our first lame phone call. Actually, I've been trying to avoid phone calls to her lately, only because it's so hard to end them. I keep wanting to say "love you, bye" like a total pussy. Or maybe I just never want to say good-bye to her.

I look around to make sure no one's watching me through the glass walls of my office before lowering my hand and checking to make sure I still have balls.

WHEN I SEE CHARLIE BOUNDING DOWN THE STEPS with Nina, he looks like a happy puppy, and I get that bittersweet feeling that's becoming so familiar to me.

"Hey, punk. What's that around your mouth?" I wipe a bit of crusty beige stuff from the corner of his lips while he grimaces and tries to push my hand away.

"Oh, that's probably hummus," Nina says.

"You got him to eat *hummus*?"

She grins. Like the cat that got the canary to eat hummus.

"I liked it with the celery and carrot sticks," my little brother states very plainly. As if it's no big deal that he's willingly consuming vegetables.

"You got him to eat celery *and* carrots? Did you check around your apartment to make sure he didn't spit them out and hide them? My dad keeps finding chunks of broccoli between the sofa cushions."

"He definitely ate it all. We started with a ranch dressing dip, and then I ran out of ranch dressing, so we switched to hummus." She holds up her hand and mouths to me in secret: *I didn't run out of ranch dressing.*

She is so fucking cute. "You got a lot of tricks up your sleeve, Miss Parks."

"They pretty much all involve ranch dressing."

"You've got a few *other* tricks as I recall," I muse, putting my arm around her waist and pulling her to me. "I've been thinking about them all day, as a matter of fact... Hi."

"Hi." She rubs my back. I kiss her, but she keeps her attention focused on Charlie.

"Gross," he mumbles, watching us. "Can Nina come to dinner?"

We walk back to my double-parked car.

"Not tonight, buddy. I'm dropping you off at Gabe's, and then I get Nina all to myself."

"For boning?"

"Hey—*what'd I say?* What'd I tell you?"

He rolls his eyes and then looks up at Nina, blushing as he quotes me: "Nina Parks is a lady. And we treat ladies with respect. We do not say words like 'boning' around her."

She doesn't laugh like she did yesterday or every other day I've known her. Just stares at the ground. Something's up.

"What'd you guys do this afternoon?"

"We just read. And watched Netflix."

"Oh yeah?" I squeeze her waist, teasing her. "You Netflix and chilled with my little brother?"

"He's reading *Matilda*," she says in a sing-song voice, eyes still fixed on Charlie.

"The girl book? That a girl gave him?"

"SHE. IS. NOT. MY. GIRLFRIEND!" Charlie stomps on the pavement with each screamed word.

"All right, all right. Settle down, punk."

. . .

THE ENTIRE RIDE, NINA AND CHARLIE TALK ABOUT Matilda, and I feel like a third wheel. She doesn't look at me when I get back to the car after taking Charlie to Gabe's door. She's not cold or anything. Just distant. And it feels like someone's been slowly stabbing at my fucking heart with a tiny dagger.

"You okay?"

She smiles and nods.

"You still want to get dinner?"

"Yeah. Definitely."

I turn off the engine again and twist around to face her. Most of my life I've been the guy who walks away as soon as I start to sense a woman is thinking about anything other than having sex with me. Now here I am, confronting her. *Take that, Dr. Glass. How you like me now?* "What is it, baby? Talk to me."

She sucks in a deep breath before speaking. Stares straight ahead. "I met someone you know. Or *knew*. At the coffee shop. After you left this morning."

"Oh yeah?" *Fuck. This can't be good.*

"I'm not sure what her name is, actually. But she knew you. I guess you must have dated her at some point."

"Uh-huh. She talked to you?"

"Yeah, you know. Not a lot."

"What'd she say?"

"Nothing bad, exactly. I mean..."

"Nina."

"It's not a big deal. We don't have to talk about it."

"I want to talk about it. I can't even guess who it was that talked to you, because—spoiler alert—I've been with a lot of women in my life. I'm not gonna sugar coat it, and I'm not gonna make any excuses. I dated those women for a little bit and then I moved on. I wasn't mean to anyone, and I did actually like them, but then I just made my exit. I made it clear to all of them up front what to expect. But I've only been with two women in the past year and a half. Sadie and you. Before Sadie, I never really committed to anyone."

"So Sadie was special?"

Be very careful what you say here... "I wanted her to be. She was my little brother's nanny. She came around at a time when we were all reeling from Clara leaving my dad and him. I wasn't used to seeing a hot chick around my family. I figured it was time for me to try to be in a relationship. I gave it a shot. It didn't work out so well. Not just the way it ended, but I probably wasn't the greatest boyfriend to Sadie. But I want to be better for you. I want to be the best for you."

She runs her hand down the side of my face and neck and then rests her head against my shoulder, and I'm dying inside.

"I'm yours now, remember? Those are the rules."

She takes a really deep breath and looks up at me optimistically. Searching my face for something that'll make her feel better somehow, and I hope to God she finds what she's looking for. She nods in agreement and then sits up. "Yeah... Hey, I know you're busy. And I totally understand if you don't have enough time to make plans, but a few months ago I booked a room at a luxury resort on Lake George for next weekend."

"For you and the principal?"

"Yeah. It would have been our three-year anniversary. I was going to surprise him, even though he hates surprises. Anyway. I didn't cancel the reservation because the librarian at our school was just raving about it, and this woman never raves about anything. Except JK Rowling and CrossFit. I was going to go by myself or ask Marnie or another girlfriend, but..."

I push the strands of hair out of her face and take her hand. "Yes."

"Really? You'd go?" It almost hurts, how surprised she is.

"Of course. Why wouldn't I?"

"I mean, it's a resort. On a lake. It just doesn't seem like the kind of thing you're into."

"I'm into *you*, Nina. If you're there, that's where I want to be."

I wish I could take a picture of her face, the way she's looking up at me right now. I want to feel like this all the time. Like the guy who put that smile on *this* woman's face.

"Good. I booked a regular hotel room with a king-size bed, but there's no view. I hope that's okay."

"Trust me, the only view I'll be looking at is your beautiful naked body."

She blushes. Thank God I can still make her blush. "Well, that will be one of the amenities you can enjoy, along with free Wi-Fi. It's for next weekend. Three nights. Friday, Saturday, and Sunday."

"Okay." I start up the engine again. "God, I can't even remember the last time I took a vacation. I need to rearrange some things, but I'm pretty sure I can make this happen."

"Okay. I've already rented a car."

"Well, darlin', you can just go ahead and cancel that

reservation. You know I've got a car. You're in it right now."

"But what if you can't make it happen?"

"Hey. I'll make it happen. I'll pay you for the room. This'll be good. This may be exactly what we need." I didn't mean to make that sound so ominous, but she seems to agree.

I COULDN'T KEEP MY HANDS OFF OF NINA ALL through dinner. When we got back to her place, we had the fastest sex we've ever had, and it wasn't even humiliating because she needed it that fast too. I think the anticipation of vacation sex has reignited something. I wish I could have stayed with her, but I've gotta get to work if I'm going to take three days off. I came to Gabe's to figure things out with him, but I keep zoning out.

"Hello?" My brother's staring at me like I'm an idiot.

"What?"

"You want Scotch or not?"

"Nah, I'm good."

"Are you? Because you seem like a moody little teenage girl to me."

"I should call Dr. Glass," I mumble, dropping my head to my hands.

"You still see her?"

"Not for a while."

"You don't need some shrink to tell you how you feel. I'll tell you how you feel. You like Nina. You're crazy about her. You've probably been falling in love with her since Day One. It's some heavy shit."

He watches me for a reaction, but I don't give him one because the words hit me in the gut. Hearing them out loud. From my brother, who knows me better than anyone.

"Here's what else you're feeling," he continues. "You're mad at Sadie for leaving, and you're mad at the guy she left you for. You're mad at Clara for leaving, and you're mad at the guy she left dad and Charlie for. But that's *their* problem. You and I may be able to help them with some things, but it's not our fault that she left and we can't change the fact that she left. You're mad that Mom died. We all are. She didn't want to leave us. We didn't want her to leave us. We all did what we could, but we couldn't beat the cancer. It's really sad. Mom wanted us to be happy. So go be happy. Finally. You deserve it. I mean, I deserve it more, but you met Nina first, so..."

I've got this stupid lump in my throat that's preventing me from telling him to fuck off, but he knows what I'm thinking.

"Whatever... Man, I didn't think there could be anything more annoying than how grumpy you were those last few months with Sadie. But then you got so fucking cheerful when you met Nina. *That* I get. *This?* This moping around when you're with the best girl you've ever known...? Jesus." He polishes off his Scotch. "Maybe you *should* be seeing Dr. Glass, because you're a fucking nut job."

Chapter Nineteen

VINCE

I can't even get her into the room fast enough.

The four-hour drive here was always fun, mostly beautiful, and fucking hell for me. Because she's wearing a flimsy little pink midriff-baring T-shirt with jean shorts and no bra. But she insisted we "wait until we get to the hotel like respectable grown-ups" before going to town on each other like horny teenagers. I would have pulled her top off in the elevator, but I don't want to get us kicked out of an upscale, old school, lakeside resort as soon as we've checked in. This ain't the W in Times Square. Also, there was an older couple in the elevator with us—I'm not an animal. Once we're in the room, though, all bets are off.

It's not that I've gotten tired of having sex with her —that seems impossible—it's just that things were getting so real back home. Three nights away from my responsibilities, with nothing but this woman on my to-do list? Heaven. Let's get down to *that* kind of business.

I'm holding both of our weekend bags in one hand,

opening the door with the other. Neither of us is talking because voices carry in the hallways of these big old buildings, but we both know exactly what's going to happen next. When the handle clicks, I hear her breath catch. I kick the door open, toss the bags on the floor, pull her inside, and press her up against the wall before it's shut again.

Her breaths are already coming so hot and heavy. "God, I want you. Vince." She drags her hands up my abs while pulling my shirt off. "I just *want* you."

"You got me, baby. You could have had me six ways to Sunday before we got to Poughkeepsie."

Her hands are all up in my hair while our tongues tangle. Moaning and arching her back as I pull her hips closer to me and slide my fingers up under that damn pink half shirt. But as soon as they find her nipples, she pushes me back. She undoes my belt and pants with a force and urgency that I haven't seen from her before, shoves them down, and has to give them a little extra help getting past the massive erection in my boxer briefs.

Her eyes are hooded and electric, and I don't even recognize her voice when she says, "Get on the bed."

Oh. Fuck. Yes. "On it." I am on that king-size bed so fast I don't even feel my feet touch the ground. But she takes her time approaching me, unbuttoning her tight little jean shorts as she kicks off her sandals, and places one pretty foot in front of the other. I lean back on my elbows and watch her shimmy out of those shorts, revealing the tiny white lace panties that must have been made for her—sweet and so sexy and designed by some genius who knew what I liked even before I did.

She climbs up on top of me with a seductive smile, straddling me and lowering herself down over my painfully hard cock, shoving me back down when I reach for her shirt.

"Come on, take it off," I plead with her.

She ignores me, kisses my chest, swirling her tongue, licking, making her way down to the waistband of my underwear. Before I know it, I'm naked and she has one hand around my shaft, taking me in her mouth, sucking and licking and savoring. She slowly moves her hand up and down, twisting and squeezing. Varying her pressure, just the way I like it. Then licks me like an ice cream cone when she cups my balls and I groan her name, reaching out to grab her hair.

"You like that?" she asks with the voice of a fallen angel.

"Yeah, I like it." I can barely speak. "I like everything you do to me."

She nibbles gently around the inside of my thighs while grabbing on to my hips, teasing me with a little intermission. She sits up and strokes the tortured length of me with the fingertips of one hand while touching herself under her shirt with the other. Teasing me.

"You little vixen. Take it off."

She makes like she's going to lift her top off but then lowers herself, gripping the base of my dick and licking her lips while holding my gaze and pressing her mouth over the head. Then she's slowly taking in as much of me as she can. I take in a sharp breath, and my whole body tenses up from my jaw down to my toes. Clench my fists. When her mouth moves back up, her hand squeezes harder. When her tongue flicks at the sweet spot under the head, I let out some kind of high-pitched sigh and then a growl as I wrap my own hand around my cock to keep it out of the way while pushing her onto her back.

I rip those fucking angel-white panties apart. Our eyes are locked on each other. I push that stupid T-shirt up out of my way so my mouth can finally consume her perfect swollen tits, my fingers rubbing her slick, engorged clit. She gasps as she pulls the shirt off over her head, and I stop to admire all of her exposed flesh—vision blurred by lust—but completely in awe of every inch of her writhing naked body.

Mine.

She manages to flip me over onto my back while I'm staring, hovers over me, and says in a voice so husky that I feel a tremor down to my bones, "I want you to come inside me." I watch her carefully lower herself onto me, her hands pressing down on my chest, mine squeezing her hips.

Last week we exchanged clean bills of health, and I tried not to think about when this would finally happen. Because I had to get a lot of work done, and I would have had a nonstop monster hard-on if I'd let myself imagine what it would feel like to have no barrier between myself and her warm, wet pussy. Anything I could have imagined would have been a far cry from the sensations I'm feeling now, and I know she can feel it too, as she lets out those sweet, hot little murmurs and sighs.

I suck in air through my teeth. "Baby, you feel so good."

She raises herself up and then lowers all the way

down on my cock. Leans back and tenses up her bent legs, squeezing me between them, slowly rocking back and forth, eyes closed. My eyes keep wanting to close, but I force myself to keep them open so I can watch this beautiful woman sway to the rhythm of me inside her. It can't be possible to adore a person any more than I adore Nina. I feel myself filling her up, the friction unbearably hot and comforting and stimulating at the same time.

I remember what she said once, about counting in French to calm herself. I try to do it in my head so I can let her enjoy bearing down on me like this, but by the time I get to *neuf,* I've got her on her back. Her calves up alongside my neck, I'm driving into her so deep she covers her mouth to muffle her screams. Skin slapping against skin has never sounded so good to me. The bed is rocking back and forth, and she reaches up to grab on to the headboard, tilting her head back and releasing a low animal sound from the depths of her throat. We're moving together with such furious grace, I don't ever want to stop.

"Fuck me harder, Vince," she hisses. "Break me apart."

Oh Christ. I take a deep breath as she lowers her feet flat on the mattress to brace herself, and I ramp things up, giving her everything I've got. My hands clasp the headboard between hers, and I thrust until I hear her cry out my name, her body tensing up beneath me, and I finally get my release. She lets go of the headboard to hold me as close to her as possible while I shudder and clench my jaw so tight to keep from saying the thing that I so desperately want to say to her.

I'm frozen in time and completely at her mercy. This is what it's felt like, ever since I met her, this desperate need to come inside her, followed by the pain of knowing that the feeling can't last forever.

She kisses my temple. My cheekbone. The side of my jaw. The top of my shoulder and then wraps her legs tight around the backs of mine, keeping me inside her.

It's perfect.

My sweet little devil.

I relax on top of her and drift off into some half-waking, half-sleep state that makes me wonder if this is all a dream.

"Is there room service?" I ask. The sun is going down, and we're still on the bed, wrapped around each other.

"I think we have to go down to the lobby bar for food at this point. We can go for a walk around the property too."

"Sounds good."

Neither of us moves.

"Eventually."

"Yeah." I nestle my face into her belly and hug her waist while she trails her fingers through my hair. "I really like this place so far," I say.

She laughs. "And to think I was worried it wouldn't be your speed."

I exhale.

"To think I was worried that *I* wouldn't be your speed."

I lift one hand up to hold hers.

"I don't know how you did it," she whispers after a long pause.

"Did what?"

"Got me to bring you home with me after knowing you for an hour. I keep thinking about it. It's like there was one moment in time that I'd be open to something like that, and you somehow found me there."

"It's funny you'd say that. Because I've been thinking that you're the one who found me. Or...you keep finding these parts of me that I didn't know existed."

She presses her lips against the top of my head, and then I feel her body tremble and know that she's laughing. "I'm sorry! It's so sweet that you said that, but—"

"Yeah yeah, I heard it as soon as I said it. You're like an adolescent boy sometimes, you know that?"

"I'm sorry. I love that you said that. I just..."

I affect a dorky voice. *"Hey, what's this thing hanging off my pelvis? I didn't even know that was there before—thanks, Nina!"*

She mimics the dorky voice. *"Hey, what's this thing behind my forehead? Oh honey, that's your frontal lobe."*

I tackle her. "You've found a side of me I didn't know I had. How's that?"

"Your good side? Finally?"

"My best side. Miss Parks, you are a Grade A smartass." I smack her butt.

She sticks the tip of her index finger in her mouth and bites it, rolling her eyeballs up like the secretly naughty good girl that she is.

"Hey..." I am about to tell her I am so fucking head over heels in love with her, but suddenly the walls shake and we hear a door slam. A man's and woman's voices heard through the wall behind our bed, somewhat hushed but definitely an argument.

We both tilt our heads toward the wall to listen because it sounds...not heated so much as *mean*. A lot of seething anger. Bad vibes.

"Should we go down and get something to eat now?" she asks.

"Yeah."

"What were you going to say?"

"I'll tell ya later."

Probably best not to say it on the first night that we're here anyway. In case shit gets awkward. Things do get awkward for everyone eventually, as our charming neighbors have reminded me.

Chapter Twenty

NINA

$\mathcal{H}$e left the Rumi book on the bedside table. For a self-proclaimed nonreader, I am impressed that he has respected the spine of the book by not leaving it open facedown. He is in the bathroom, done showering. But I can't help but pick up the book to check to see if it looks read. He hasn't said anything since I gave it to him, which is fine—it's hard to talk about poetry. You either get it or you don't. I can tell immediately that every page has been looked at. Flipping through it, I see that he has underlined many sentences from the introduction by the translator and earmarked one page.

I hear him talking in the bathroom, probably on the phone. I have to see what page he earmarked. I flip to it and see that it's my favorite poem, a tiny one. *"The minute I heard my first love story..."* and he wrote in pencil, on the page: **_THIS_**

I put the book back the way it was on the bedside table, smiling and feeling warm all over.

Yes. This.

The bathroom door opens. Vince walks out wearing nothing but his swim trunks, looking all shiny and new, and I feel warm all over in a completely different way. But when I hear Charlie's voice through his phone, I sit up straight and get into Miss Parks-mode. I'm wearing a flimsy sundress over my bikini and need to make sure I don't accidentally expose too much of myself.

"Show me the room!" Charlie says. Vince turns his phone around to give him a 360 of the room. I wave at Charlie's little face on the screen. "Oh hey!"

"Morning!"

Vince brings the phone over to me on the bed. His dad's face pops into view.

"Hey, Nina. We could use your help with something."

"Hi, Neil."

Vince gives me his phone to hold and immediately slides his hand up my dress, between my legs. I try to push his hand away without his dad noticing.

"Charlie here is going to his friend's birthday party this afternoon, and we haven't got her a present yet. He wants to get her a book. Thoughts? She's eight."

"Oh Charlie, is this the girl who gave you *Matilda*?"

"Yes." He frowns. And blushes.

"Did you finish reading it?"

"Yeah, I liked it."

"Well, maybe you should give her one of your favorite books."

"She's already read *Harry Potter*."

"Okay, what else do you like? What other books do you re-read when you get the chance?"

"*Holes. Phantom Tollbooth,* I guess."

"Great books! I love *Holes,* but since I don't know the girl, it might be a little dark for her. You should get her *Phantom Tollbooth,* and then you can talk about it."

Vince is snickering, and Neil rolls his eyes.

"I think you should talk to your girlfriend about holes," Vince says to Charlie.

"Oh my God." I punch his bicep. "You dork."

"She's not my girlfriend!"

"Where's Gabe when you need him?" Vince shakes his head.

"Okay, we gotta go to the bookstore. Thanks, Nina. Have fun, you guys. Stay outta trouble."

"Not a chance."

"Have fun at the party, Charlie!"

Vince ends the call and tosses the phone away before I can stop him from pulling off my dress. My lukewarm complaints about how we have to get out to enjoy the sun and let housekeeping clean the room go ignored.

It took another hour to get out of the hotel room because we both had to ensure that the other was thoroughly covered in sunscreen. My body has never felt so adored and attended to, and seeing the man Eve referred to as "Mr. Seriously Sexy" behave like an insatiable teenager at times is flattering to say the least.

The resort is fully booked, so it is not surprising to find that all of the recliners around the pools are taken by the time we circle the area. I notice about fifty different women of all ages—moms and grandmas, women on their honeymoons—checking out the delicious man I'm holding hands with. I do not blame them. He looks super fine in his swim trunks, tank top, and aviators.

"Let's go down to the waterfront. There's a beach, right?"

"Yeah," I say. "Let's do that." He could have said *Let's go to hell—it's warm there, right?* And I would have just stared at his butt and said, *Yeah. Let's do that.*

"Hang on. I wanna get a picture of us with this view. Look at that. It's gorgeous here."

It really is. It's a beautiful day, and the location of this resort, in the Adirondacks, on the lake, is perfect. It's hard to believe I made these reservations for Russell and me. He probably would have insisted on spending the days seeking out antiques and dining. And I would have made myself believe that I like it.

I feel self-conscious when Vince holds up his camera to take a picture of us. This is the first time we've taken an "usie" together. He leans in, cheek pressed up against mine, and takes three shots. He looks at the pictures. "Damn. We look good together."

Damn. We do look good together. He texts me the pictures, and I try to ignore the sinking feeling that those will one day be the only evidence of our summer together. I shake it off and let him lead me down to the beach, where there are slightly fewer people for some reason.

"Why would anyone want to sit around a pool when they could be by the lake?" he wonders aloud.

"I have no idea."

We place our towels and things on two side-by-side patio lounge chairs and look out at the lake.

"You want to go in the water?"

"Not yet. Let's get some sun first."

"I was hoping you'd say that." He lies back and closes his eyes.

It isn't anywhere near as humid here as it is in the city now, and I love it. I find myself wondering if we can squeeze in another weekend getaway before the summer is over.

The relative quiet is suddenly disturbed when a woman squeals as a man picks her up and hangs her over his shoulder and then drops her into the lake. She splashes him before standing up, casually rearranging her tight little bikini over her lady bits.

As they walk back up the beach, I realize they're heading for the two empty lounge chairs next to mine. They both stare at us as they slow their pace.

It takes my brain about five long seconds to recognize the man as my former fiancé. He looks like a Mad Man-era hot dad in his slim red swim trunks. Or a vampire principal from a CW show (you know, the kind that can go out in broad daylight). He is frowning and wrinkling his forehead as he approaches, straining to see me in the sun and also probably formulating a strategy for how to deal with me.

The woman reaches for the towel on the chair next to mine, turning her toned backside to me as she dries off.

I realize my mouth is hanging open. Time has slowed down, and I am not aware of anything else in the world except this woman who's standing next to me.

I have had this image of Sadie the nanny in my mind. In my mind, she is blonde, blue-eyed, buxom, with creamy skin and she smells like strawberries. A sexed-up Julie Andrews. Essentially, the opposite of me (a *not* sexed-up Julie Andrews)—although I do sometimes smell like strawberries.

The real Sadie is indeed blonde, bleached with hot pink streaks in her hair, a lean, lithe, yet somehow also infuriatingly curvy body, and an elaborate lower back tattoo that basically looks like an exposed black lace thong. I mean. I could see why guys would find that attractive. But why not just wear a black lace thong? They always end up creeping out of the top of jeans anyway. Wouldn't it look dumb if she wore patterned boy shorts one day and then the tattoo peeked out behind that? And that's when I realize: *she doesn't wear underwear*. Of course. Why would twenty-two-year-old blonde tattooed Sadie wear underwear? Therein lies the main difference between Sadie and me. You take one look at her and start obsessing about her underpants situation. Take one look at me and you think: *I bet she's really good at reading Captain Underpants books out loud.*

I feel sick. It's not a judgment on Sadie. It's the insidious realization that the two men I've most recently had sex with have also recently had sex with this super sexy sexbot. I had somehow managed not to think about it for thirty glorious seconds, and now I can't imagine ever *not* thinking about it. I don't have self-esteem issues, but let's get real here: I could totally understand why a man would want to procreate with me, because obviously I will be an amazing mom. But why would anyone want to have recreational sex with me after doing it with her? That must be like going from snorting cocaine to drinking a warm can of Coke. There's no way Vince wanted to have sex with me for any reason other than revenge. It doesn't make sense.

As he towels off, Russell says, as casually as if he were greeting a stranger, "Hello, Nina."

Sadie turns her head to look at me just as Vince raises himself up on one elbow, shielding his eyes from the sun with one hand.

"Vince?" Her voice is deep and Slavic. Also not what I expected. "What the fuck?"

"Shit," he mutters. He sits up and reaches for my hand.

"Wait, what?" Russell's voice remains ostensibly calm, but I can see and hear the tension. "What's going on here?"

I refuse to feel like a couple of kids who have been caught fooling around under the bleachers, because that is the tone he's using right now.

"Hello, Russell," I say. "Fancy meeting you here."

"Wait, so...that's *your* Nina?" Sadie says to Russell. "Because *that's* my Vince."

"Not anymore," Vince says, squeezing my hand.

Russell holds his hand up in the air. "What is happening here?"

"Not much. What's happening with you?" Vince removes his sunglasses and looks Russell straight in the eyes.

"Nina, did you follow us here?"

"Are you kidding me? Did *you* follow *us*? Because I made reservations like three months ago. You can ask the front desk."

Russell's jaw tightens, but his shoulders relax. "Well, so did I."

A look passes between us, barely anything, but we silently realize that we both made surprise reservations for our three-year anniversary here. Because we both heard the librarian rave about it.

"Imagine that," I say.

"So...wait," says Sadie, dramatically rubbing her temples. "So you guys are together? How did that happen?"

"It's really none of your business," mumbles Vince.

"You sure about that? Because it seems like it has a lot to do with me and Russell. Don't you think, Russ?"

Russ? He doesn't let anyone call him Russ. He is so not a Russ.

He considers before responding and then comes up with this jewel: "I think it's their business how they choose to deal with things."

Vince guffaws. "Wow. You really are a principal."

"Okay," says Sadie. "Okay. Whatever. So you guys are together, and you're here and we're here. Okay. Hi, I'm Sadie," she says to me, extending her hand.

I shake her hand. "Nice to meet you, Sadie. I'm Nina."

Vince and Russell just stare each other down, and I feel like I'm in *Call of the Wild* for a second.

"So anyway. Good to see you, Vince." Sadie sits down at the edge of the lounge chair and proceeds to towel-dry her hair. "How's Charlie?"

"Fine. He's great, actually."

"I miss him."

"Oh yeah?"

"I bet he doesn't even remember me."

"He remembers you. He missed you for like a week, but he's okay."

"I wish he had a phone so I could text him."

"Yeah, well. He's eight."

"Right. God forbid a Devlin man should keep in touch with a girl."

"Right. *That's* the point."

"We should get back to the room," Russell states as he's folding up his towel.

"Yeah. Hey, babe?" Sadie says to *Russ*. "When's our dinner reservation for? Seven?"

"Yes."

"You guys should join us. We got a table at the restaurant here. Out on the deck."

"I'm sure they have other plans, babe," says Russell.

"Not for dinner," someone says, and I am shocked to realize that it is Vince. "Right, baby? We'd love to join you guys. Thanks."

I feel Vince tighten his grip on my hand briefly. "Sure, why not," I mumble.

"Cool. It'll be good to catch up. Clear the air and all that, yeah?" She picks up her flip-flops and starts to walk away with Russell. "See you there at seven!"

When they are out of sight, Vince lies back and covers his face, laughing. "What the fuck just happened?"

"Why did you say yes?"

He sits back up and takes my hands in his. "If you don't want to go, we won't go. That guy was just so uncomfortable, I couldn't help it."

"Vince. I still have to work with him every day

starting in September. He's my supervisor." I feel sick again. And suddenly angry. Not at them—at Vince. "Is this still all about getting back at Russell for you?"

He seems genuinely shocked by this question. "Are you seriously asking me that?"

"Yes, I'm asking you, instead of wondering about it silently to myself until I throw up."

"Nina. It hasn't been about that since I met you. It's definitely not about that now. I just don't like the guy, and I wanted to piss him off. I have a thing about principals. Baby, I'm sorry. We don't have to go to dinner with them. We can leave if you want to." He rubs his lips together, thinking. "I can try to find another resort around here. I know a guy who owns a resort at Lake Placid. It's not as nice as this, but..."

"No, I like it here. I don't want to leave. They should leave."

"I agree." He moves over to my lounge chair and wraps his arms around me. "Come on. Don't you think it would be fun? They're the weirdest fucking couple ever, and we're amazing. It's kind of hilarious."

"Yeah, but...I just don't want to make this about *them*."

"Nothing's about them. Everything's about us. Come on, it'll be fun. If it's not, we'll leave."

I wrinkle my nose. "It is so weird seeing them together."

"Right? But what's weirder is seeing you and him together. I mean, Sadie's got daddy issues, but you...?"

"I know. I'm not going to explain it again. It made sense when it made sense."

He kisses my shoulder and then wipes his mouth

because sunscreen doesn't taste good. He puts his aviators back on, resting his hand on my thigh. He's almost always touching me. I stare at his beautiful face. I love that face. I want that face all up in my face. When he looks over at me, I can tell he's feeling the exact same rush as I am all of a sudden.

"Is it just me," I whisper, "or are you also feeling super horny right now?"

"Race you back to the room." He hops up, and we speed-walk past families and other couples. "Felt good being outside for a minute, though. This is a special place."

"Yeah. I'm really glad we came."

Chapter Twenty-One

NINA

I can't say that I've ever gone into a double-date situation with high hopes, but my ambitious goal for tonight is merely to suffer through it without anyone getting punched or having a drink thrown in their face. Having packed for a romantic sexy weekend getaway with Vince, all of my outfits were selected with the objective of inspiring him to rip them off me. For this dinner, I've chosen to wear the most conservative of options—a pretty red flowery dress and sandals. Vince has ostensibly spent exactly zero seconds deciding what to wear or worrying about what the next couple of hours of our life will be like.

"You ready to go?" he asks as he sends off an email and slides his phone into his pocket. I stare at his hands. His beautiful, slightly rough, capable hands. I want them on me. "You look beautiful. I love you in red."

"Thanks. Let's get this over with, I guess."

He takes my hand and kisses my cheek. "I think this

is gonna be fun. Not as fun as what we did on the couch this afternoon, but you know. Entertaining."

I grab him and hug him. He hasn't proved to be much of a hugger before now, but I just want to press my body up against his and breathe him in. He gently rubs my back, and I feel the masculine warmth of him down to my bones. The epic montage of sex this afternoon was a chaos of disparate emotions that I don't have the time or space to sort through, but right now I feel dangerously attached to him.

There's nothing like having a Them to make you feel like an Us.

We're both startled to hear the door to the room next to us slam shut. We were treated to the muffled sounds of the couple going at it off and on for the past hour, and I mean "going at it" in the bad way. Not the way Vince and I were going at it. That was the good way. The really good way. And we were not quiet.

Vince's hand is on the doorknob, but he waits to turn it because we hear the adjacent door open and shut again and a man's voice hiss, "Sadie! Wait for me!"

Our wide eyes lock together. My hand covers my mouth as he starts laughing.

"Oh shit," he says quietly.

"Oh no. We should wait—"

He opens the door and ushers me out into the hallway. Sadie is waiting at the elevator, hands on her hips, foot tapping. Russell strides toward her, his body rigid. If Sadie's got daddy issues, she clearly wants a spanking. And a summer cold. Because she's wearing what appears to be a large napkin tied around her torso and white shorts that confirm my suspicion that she goes commando. I guess I shouldn't talk. I was barely wearing anything when we drove up here. What is it about Vince that just makes women want to expose themselves?

Vince and I are about ten feet behind Russell. When Sadie looks back, her petulant face falls, and then her eyes narrow.

"Hey, guys. I was just rushing downstairs so we wouldn't have to keep you waiting."

"So considerate, as always," says Vince.

Russell slows his pace and turns his head. "Oh hello."

"Small world. I guess we've got the room next to yours," says Vince.

I watch Sadie's face and read her thoughts: *What the fuck? Fuck, they heard us fighting. Fuck, we heard them fucking. Fuck, I should have worn an even smaller napkin.* She reaches out for Russell's hand. "Small world, indeed. Still getting my head wrapped around this whole situation. You guys have a nice afternoon? We found the most adorable antique stores. Russ really hit the jackpot."

"It wasn't exactly a windfall, but I found the perfect vintage brass lamp for my home office and a copy of an old Herbie Hancock record that's in much better condition than the one I have now."

"Oh yeah? Which album?" Vince seems genuinely curious.

"*Speak Like a Child.* It's not one of his best-known."

"Yeah, I've got that one. Transitional. I love that album—Mickey Roker on drums. Great drummer."

As we all step into the elevator, Russell gives Vince

the once-over. "You like Roker? He played on my favorite Dizzy Gillespie album."

"*Big 4?*"

"How'd you guess?"

"I dunno, instinct. 'September Song.'"

"Yes! That's my favorite track."

While they continue geeking out over classic jazz artists and vinyl, Sadie leans back and widens her eyes at me, smirking. I smile and shrug and wonder if maybe this dinner won't be so terrible after all. Maybe we'll all get along. We definitely have the potential to, so why not?

Russell certainly looks more easygoing than he used to. He's wearing dark jeans with cuffs and a black T-shirt. She must be dressing him. The most casual garments I'd ever seen him in were chinos and summer weight button-down shirts. He's even wearing contacts. He once told me he'd rather be blind than stick contact lenses on his eyeballs. I guess he'd rather stick contact lenses on his eyeballs than not get to see Sadie's tramp stamp up close.

VINCE AND I SIT ACROSS FROM SADIE AND RUSSELL AT a table on the deck. We have a panoramic view of the lake and mountains, and it has taken us all about two minutes to power through a bottle of red after Vince cryptically toasted "to fate" and Sadie toasted "to karma."

"So, what have you guys been up to?" Sadie asks. "Just hanging out?"

"Oh, you know," Vince says. "Hanging out, staying

in, going out, *eating* out... Attending to certain neglected areas in Nina's life." He looks right at Russell as he says this. I pinch his thigh. "How about you guys?"

I don't think Russell got the reference, and I'm glad.

"Same, really," Sadie says. "We eat out practically every night. He's developed a taste for it." She glances at me with her eyebrow slightly arched.

"We went to a new tapas restaurant in Queens last week. Fantastic."

Oh, Russ. So blissfully unaware of anything outside your own limited interests.

Sadie, on the other hand. Her eyes are always wide open and watching everything. But it's not a doe-eyed interest in the world. It's plain to me that she's studying everyone. Figuring things out, deciding what to do, how to play it. It must be exhausting.

"It *was* fantastic. Russ has really opened up my palate. And I always thought I had a good tongue."

Vince rolls his eyes. His hand has been on my thigh ever since we sat down. He gives me a little squeeze.

"Actually, babe...the nose and the mind are more involved than the tongue in an evolved palate."

Sadie playfully sticks her tongue out at Russell, revealing a tongue stud. So she has *that* going for her too. Having sex with me after having sex with her must be like riding the world's greatest roller coaster and then hopping onto a rickety old merry-go-round.

I look around for the waiter and signal that we need more wine.

"Vince. Sadie tells me you're a Realtor."

"I'm a commercial real estate broker."

"That must be interesting."

"It can be. I just closed a deal on a gorgeous location in Brooklyn Heights, for a big up-and-coming chef. It should be an exciting new restaurant in a few months."

"That so? Which chef would that be?"

"Clive Court. He owns Succulent, in the East Village."

"Oh sure." Russell nods and wipes his mouth with his napkin, swallowing his buttered bread. "We went there last year." He gestures toward me. "Not my favorite."

"I remember liking it a lot. Beautiful space."

"Wow, you finally closed that deal, huh? He was working on that back when we were together," she says to me.

"I think you mean back when you and Russell were together." Vince sounds so lighthearted, it barely registers as a dig.

Sadie smiles and tilts her head. "You're right. You were so busy at that point, you barely had time for me."

"Actually, you were the one who was always 'busy with the new job.'"

"I was. Brooks was a real handful in the beginning."

Russell clears his throat. "It's true, actually. He was getting into a lot of trouble at school, but Sadie's been a good influence on him. She really keeps him in line."

"I'll bet he doesn't even realize how much. Poor kid," Vince mutters.

The middle-aged hippie lady at the table next to ours keeps looking back at us, and I would not be at all surprised if she got up to burn sage all around us to raise our vibrations and clear the air. I would welcome that. Until then, I will have to do my part.

I pat Vince's hand and smile at Sadie. "Brooks sounds interesting. How old is he?"

"He's ten. He's a great kid, actually. Really smart. You want to see pictures?"

"Of course." *I bet he's a South Side Soc.*

"He's a really handsome little devil."

"Complicated boy. But very shrewd," says Russell. "Sadie speaks highly of your little brother," he offers to Vince.

"Good" is his reply.

Sadie pulls out her phone and smiles innocently as she swipes through some photos. "His parents are super busy, but they're all in Hawaii this week. Here, this is a great shot of him." She turns her phone so I can see it and slowly swipes once she's thoroughly enjoyed seeing the look on my face as I get a glimpse of the picture of her and Vince kissing each other. That photo is replaced by one of a dark-haired boy who's looking up at the camera like he's mesmerized by the person taking the picture.

"He is handsome," I manage to say with barely any volume. "He looks like an old soul." *And a total Bob Sheldon from The Outsiders.*

"That's what I always say!" she exclaims, putting the phone away. "It's too bad he didn't get to be in your class." She nudges Russell. "I bet he would have liked her, huh?"

"And vice versa," he quips. "Nina always did have a soft spot for the bad boys. Tell me, Vince—which college did you go to?"

"Well, I used to tell people that I graduated from the College of Hard Knocks with a double major in

Fuck You, if I got the sense they were being condescending. But since this is such a friendly double date…"
He doesn't say anything else, just finishes his glass of
wine.

"Vince is one of the smartest people I've ever met,"
I say, sounding just a tiny bit defensive.

Vince turns his head to me, grinning. "Yeah?"

"Yeah. You've got a sharp mind. Lightning fast,
really."

"Wow," says Russell. "Sharp *and* lightning fast. That
is impressive."

"And it's not even the most impressive thing about
him," I say, looking directly at Russell and Sadie.

Vince is quietly laughing and holding my hand, but
it's the second and third glasses of wine that get me
through dinner.

AFTER SADIE INSISTS WE ALL ORDER DESSERT AND
coffee, she starts telling a seemingly innocuous story
about Charlie that has Vince fuming. It seems to me
that she is subtly egging him on, and they sound like a
divorced couple with a child. And I just want to get the
flork out of here.

"That's not how it went down at all," he says
through clenched teeth.

"You aren't actually suggesting that it's *my* fault he
broke the TV?"

"No, I just don't think you handled it in the best way
afterwards."

"Well, you weren't my employer. Your dad was, and
he didn't have any complaints."

"No, he just got high blood pressure a few months after hiring you."

"Oh. My. God. Vince. Can I talk to you in private?" She pushes her chair back.

"Nope."

She looks directly at me.

I say in the gentlest, most easygoing voice I can conjure up, "Go ahead. It's fine."

He searches my eyes before coming to a decision. "Okay." He nods toward the doors to the lobby. "We'll be right over there. Be right back." Vince kisses my cheek and slowly follows Sadie out of the restaurant, passing the confused busboy who is returning with our coffee.

Russell and I are silent and refrain from making eye contact until we are alone at the table.

"How are your parents?"

"They're great."

"Good."

"They stopped by my apartment, actually, on their way to Florida. They met Vince. They loved him."

"How nice."

"How's your early midlife crisis going?"

"It was going great until you showed up."

"Oh really? That's not what it looked or sounded like to me."

"Looks and sounds can be deceiving."

"Right. Like when you *look* like a totally nice guy and I *hear* you say that you love me, but then you go and—"

"Nina—let's not."

"Fine with me."

"We're almost out of the woods here. Let's just give

those two the opportunity to let off some steam, and then we can all go back to our romantic weekends."

"Fantastic idea."

After a beat, he says, "Interesting that you and I had the same idea. For this resort."

"Yeah. I'm glad we both ended up here with the right person."

"You think so? Sadie has told me a few things about your gentleman friend. I hope you know who you've gotten yourself involved with."

Do not let that get into your head. Do not let it get into your head. "Oh yes, I am in this with eyes wide open."

"And legs too, apparently."

"Abso-fucking-lutely."

"Ahhh, you swear now. What a charming surprise."

"Sometimes. Just for the summer. I do a lot of things that feel good now, as I am quite certain you do too."

"Well, good for you. But I doubt your boy has told you everything about himself."

"Did you know that people can have sex standing up —*against a wall?* And in the shower! And *from behind?* And with the woman on top, facing away from the—"

"I don't know if you think you're being funny, but you are not."

"I don't know if you realize you don't have a sense of humor, but you don't."

"Okay. I was hoping we could both be adults about this, but..."

If he wants to believe I'm the nonadult here, that is fine with me. I snort-laugh. In a really mature way.

"Believe it or not, Nina, I do care about you. As a co-worker and as a friend."

I can't even snort-laugh at those words. He actually seems to believe them.

"I just don't want to see you get hurt. This thing with this guy is just a rebound. It won't end well."

This is a summer of firsts. I've never been gobs-macked before. I've always loved that term, never felt it. I am suddenly, completely smacked in the gob.

"Do you honestly not realize that you're the bad guy in this scenario?"

He nods. "I'm fine with you thinking that."

"Wow. Fantastic. Big of you."

"The truth is, Nina, and I'm just going to say it now...since you wouldn't hear it that day when you tossed my belongings out the window—you ended our relationship long before I did."

"Uh-huh. Remind me how I did that?"

I see his Adam's apple bob up and down once. His voice is strained. He speaks so quietly that my ears strain to hear him, even though I know exactly what he's going to say before he says it: "You were never in love with me. You never really wanted to marry me. You just thought you should." He doesn't look at me. He doesn't have to. He knows he's right. He knows I know it's true.

I feel the tip of my nose tingling, and my eyes get watery. For the first time in ages, I remember why I had so much respect for Russell. He can read people. He knows how to treat children who are angry or sad or hurting, when to point things out, when to let them figure things out for themselves. I didn't think he was very good at dealing with grown-ups. Until now.

"Russell..." I have to clear my throat. "I just hope

you're happy now. I really do. I don't want things to be weird for us when school starts."

"Same here." He doesn't say if he's happy or not, and I really can't tell either way. "But I'm not kidding about that guy. He's got a lot going for him, obviously, but there's some unresolved anger there and it's as plain as the tattoos on his arm."

I don't disagree, but I have to say something. "I love the tattoos on his arm."

"I'm sure." He lifts his coffee cup to his lips and says with a smirk, "I got a tattoo."

"Shut up. You did not."

"I did. Just a little one. I can't show it to you. It's in a private place, obviously."

I have to ask. "What's it of?"

"A line from an Amy Winehouse song."

If I were drinking my coffee, I would have done a spit-take. "It is not."

"It is. Sadie got me into her. I can't believe I never listened to her before. She moves me in ways that...I never expected."

I don't ask him if he means Amy Winehouse or Sadie. He seems just as mystified by everything that's going on as I am right now, and all I can think about is whether or not Vince is in the lobby feeling moved in ways that I could never move him.

Chapter Twenty-Two

VINCE

Okay, so this dinner hasn't been as entertaining or satisfying as I had expected it would be. All I can think about is how I'm going to have to do something pretty fucking awesome to make things up to Nina. Even as Sadie paces around in front of me here in this corner of the lobby, trying as always to make everything about her.

"Where the fuck do you get off being so rude to me, huh?"

"Keep it down—this is a nice place."

"Really? You think *I'm* the one behaving inappropriately?"

"Yeah. I do."

"Seriously—how the hell did you end up with Russell's ex?" She taps at her temple, so condescending. "Do you even see how crazy that shit is?"

"I am aware that it seems like a bad idea, but I also know it's the best decision I've ever made."

"You're talking about the world's shortest list of good decisions."

"Not denying that."

"Okay, but you have to at least tell me—who sought who out? Did *she* find *you*?"

"No."

She nods once. "That's what I thought. A revenge fuck."

"It is so much more than that, and I think that's obvious to you or you wouldn't be trying so hard to get to me."

Her eyelids flutter. Her posture changes. And I know she's about to attempt to manipulate me, but I'm so immune to this shit now it isn't even funny. I don't know how it's possible that I wasted so much time with someone who brings out the worst in me, now that I'm with someone who brings out the best.

"Vince, I really was hoping that we could all get along tonight. I wanna clear the air. Can't we be friends?"

"No. We can't."

"Well, I want to see Charlie."

"You can't."

"You can't stop me."

"Yes, I can."

She crosses her arms at her chest. "So what do you think of Russ? You like him, don't you?"

"I can see why *you* like him."

"And I can see why you like *her*."

"Fantastic. Are we done here?"

She ignores the question completely, slides her hands down her midriff, and slips them into the front pockets of her shorts, hunching over a bit so I can see her cleavage. I know that move. I fell for that move over a year ago. It does nothing for me now. "So, he asked me to move in with him."

"The principal?"

She nods. "Before the school year starts up again. I don't know if I should. Everything's happening so fast."

"Sometimes good things happen fast."

"So you think I should?"

"I think it makes no difference to me if you do or don't, and you've got no business asking my opinion."

"It's just, you know. What if I give up my room at Darcy's place to move in with him, and then he realizes this was just a rebound? I'll never find as good a place with as cheap a rent as I have now." She bites her lower lip, pretending to be confused. I almost hate her.

I think of Nina and take a deep breath to calm my nerves so I don't make a scene. "Who knows what'll happen. You either enjoy what you have right now or you don't, I guess. Personally, I'm actually grateful that you ended up with Russell, or I probably never would have found Nina. So thanks."

She looks at me, her lower lip quivering, and then her eyes harden. "Yeah, I feel the same way. If you hadn't made it so unbearable for me to keep being Charlie's nanny toward the end there, I wouldn't have gotten my new job and I wouldn't have met Russ. So thanks for being such a moody dick all the time."

"It was my pleasure." I grin. She smiles. It's probably as close as we're ever going to get to a truce. I start to turn to go back into the restaurant. "Just stay away from Charlie. I mean it."

I GAVE OUR WAITER MY CREDIT CARD TO PAY FOR THE table before returning from the lobby and managed to get through dessert without showing any hint of emotion toward Sadie. But she had to get in one last dig about how "fascinating" it is that Nina and I got together, and I slammed my water glass down on the table. It startled Nina. I saw how Russell gave her a look afterwards, and Sadie had this smug expression on her face. *There it is,* she was thinking. *I knew it.* I had to get us out of there immediately.

Now we're back in our room, and Nina's barely said two words to me. The TV is on, probably more to block out any sounds that Sadie and Russell will make when they get back to their room—but also to give her something to look at other than me.

I feel sick.

"I shouldn't have agreed to go to dinner with them," I say.

She looks down at her hands. "I'm glad we did, to be honest."

"You are?"

She nods. "Mostly. I had a pretty good little talk with Russell when you were in the lobby."

I feel my ears getting warm. "Yeah?"

"Not a lot. I just...I think it'll be okay for us to work together. I'm not mad at him anymore. I don't think he's mad at me."

"That's good. I'm glad. Can we turn off the TV?"

She picks up the remote and turns it off.

I sit on the sofa beside her, taking her hands in

mine. We both jump a little when we hear doors and drawers in the next room slamming shut.

"Uh-oh," she mumbles. "How'd your talk with Sadie go?"

"It was...mildly dysfunctional."

"She's very...shrewd."

"If by that you mean 'manipulative,' then yes. She is."

"I think Russell's really taken with her."

I exhale slowly. "I do too. I'm so sorry I let her get to me like that. Slamming the glass down, and..."

"I saw what she was doing. Trying to provoke you. I don't blame you."

"Still, I should have been able to control myself better."

She gives me a quick glance, and I have no idea what it means.

I can hear Sadie yelling behind the wall, so clearly, "Oh my God just give me *one* minute!" I can't imagine the principal's still going to want her to move in with him, but maybe he likes the drama. Some guys do. You never know how people are going to respond to each other. Maybe I wouldn't have found Nina so appealing if I'd met her a couple of years ago, although that's hard to imagine.

She's watching the door to our room, as if she's afraid one of them will knock on it. We hear Russell say, "Just *come on*," and then a few seconds later their door shuts and Sadie is stomping past our room.

"We're leaving!" she yells out. "Enjoy the rest of your stay!"

Russell shushes her.

Nina's holding her breath until we hear their foot-steps go all the way to the end of the hall. It's quiet again.

"I actually feel bad for the guy."

She nods. "I think I need to go to sleep," she says, sounding genuinely apologetic. "Sorry. It's just hitting me how tired I am."

"It's nine thirty."

"I know. I just...I haven't gotten that much sleep since I met you." She grins. "I'm not complaining, believe me. I guess it's just catching up with me. During the school year I'm always in bed by ten, you know."

Those words, *During the school year*. She might as well say: *When you're not a part of my life*.

She puts her hand on my cheek and kisses me. "Do you mind?"

"Course not. I'll read in bed beside you. If you don't mind me keeping the lamp on."

She smiles. "I don't. I'd like that, actually."

It's the first time we've gone to bed without fucking first. Although, yes, we did it multiple times today already, but still. I'm all for domesticity, if that's what this is a preview of, but something ain't right.

When I wake up, Nina is standing at the window, looking out at the rain.

Perfect.

"Morning."

She keeps looking out the window. "It's raining," she says ominously.

"I'm sure it won't last long."

"My weather app disagrees with you."

"Sounds like you should come back to bed."

She turns to face me and half smiles. "I was thinking we should get breakfast in the lobby while they're still serving it."

"Okay. I'll get up. Can we bring it back here?"

"Probably. If that's what you want."

"Is that what *you* want?"

"I guess. Let's see what it's like when we're down there."

"Yeah. Let's do that."

Fuck me. It's like we just fast-forwarded three years into the relationship. Not that I'd really know what that's like. Right now, I would do anything to take back everything that happened from the second Sadie invited us to dinner until now. Except for the sex part.

WE BRING OUR BREAKFAST BACK UP TO THE ROOM, and Nina has her Rainy Day playlist streaming on her Spotify app. I hate listening to music from a phone, but it's so cute that she has playlists based on weather that I do not complain.

I stare at her as she eats her buttered toast, watching her lick her lips, and even though we're at a resort in upstate New York, this feels like home to me. I just don't know how to say that to her without it sounding totally cornball gross.

She looks up and sees me staring at her. "What?" She wipes her lips with the back of her hand.

"You know, if you ever want to stay in and chill—I mean, back home—just tell me. I'd be fine with that."

"Really?"

"Hell yeah, really."

"I don't want to bore you."

"Well, I don't want to tire you out."

"You don't. Not at all."

"Good. You don't bore me."

"But I'm such a lame nerd."

"You're my favorite lame nerd ever. I totally geek out over you."

This seems to make her pretty happy. "I did bring a little something along, just in case it rained." She gets up for her purse.

"If it's handcuffs, you are officially *not* lame. Not even close."

She reaches inside the bag and fishes around for something, shaking her head.

"I will settle for a can of whipped cream."

She shakes her head again.

"It's gummy bears, isn't it?"

"I do have a baggie full of them. You want some?"

"Maybe later."

She pulls out a deck of cards and holds them up. "Still lame?"

"Depends. What'd you have in mind? Go Fish? Slapjack?"

"Possibly. Or…"

.   .   .

After beating my ass at Blackjack twenty times, she suggests Texas Hold'em. I tell her I'd rather play Go Fish, because it's something I play regularly with Charlie and if she beats me at that, I'll feel like I can retain a little dignity. More so than if she wins at poker. After last night, if I can't leave this place with my dignity intact and a sense that I actually deserve this woman, then I don't even want to know what that'll do to me.

Chapter Twenty-Three

NINA

"Well, that's a shame," I say, shuffling the deck of cards on top of the bedspread.

"Why's that?" Vince asks, rubbing his hands together in anticipation. "Don't tell me you suck at Go Fish."

"Nope. I was going to suggest a game of Strip Poker. But now you've got me all excited about Go Fish."

He tightens his jaw, grinning. "Oh, you little tease." He swipes the cards off the bed, knocks the empty plates to the carpet, and lunges toward me.

I squeal, even though he's doing exactly what I need him to do. This quiet tension that's been building inside me since last night needs to be released...transformed... and he is surely the most adept, sexiest alchemist alive. He scoops me up in his arms and carries me...to the dresser across the room. *Oh God, yes.* The one piece of furniture in this room we haven't done it on yet.

He is rough and animalistic, looking up at me with

eyes full of heat as he sets me down on top of the dresser. I guess *not* having sex with me last night was harder on him than I thought it would be, because he is...hard. Wow, he is so hard against my leg. While he kisses my neck, I try to unbutton his jeans—but he pushes my hand away, pulls his shirt off over his head, and drops his pants in one swift movement.

I knew from the moment I first saw him that he could get naked fast, but that was the fastest I've seen him do it so far. Before I have a chance to reach for his cock, he growls and yanks my lounge pants and panties down, the shock making me jump a little so he can pull them off past my ass and to the floor. I start to raise my arms so he can remove my top and bra, but he is already pushing inside me. I gasp, but I am already so wet for him, it only hurts for a second. And once he's thrusting into me, the dresser slamming against the wall, his hands holding me in place by the hips, I forget everything.

There was no last night, there's no rain, there are no questions, there is no end to this summer, there is only this.

His breathy grunting, the heat between us, the savage need to be a part of each other in a way that's so uncomplicated, the only word I can remember now is *yes*.

Yes.

Yes.

Blissed out after showering, tangled up in each other on the bed, I feel emboldened enough to risk the question.

"Can I ask you something?"

"Anything."

"Is there anything else that I should know about you? Anything you're afraid of telling me?"

He doesn't seem particularly surprised by this line of questioning. "What do you mean?"

"I don't want you to get upset."

"I'm not."

"When you were out in the lobby, Russell mentioned something..."

"That sounds promising," he mumbles.

"Something Sadie told him."

"I knew it. I knew something was up."

"I just don't like him knowing something that I don't. If that's the case."

"Yeah. Fucking principals. You know, when I was in high school, the guy was always trying to 'make an example' out of me."

"The principal?"

"He was a dick. I know they aren't all like that, but I guess I have a bias against them. She knew that, too. I'm not saying that's why she started up with him, but... I wouldn't put it past her." The way he says "she" when he's referring to Sadie. He can't even speak her name right now.

"Wait, so it has to do with the principal of *your* high school?"

"Not exactly." He sighs.

Here we go...

He sits up and gazes down at my face. I'm sure I look so worried. I sit up too, pull my legs up to my chest, and hug them in. I give him a slow, reassuring blink to let him know he can tell me anything.

"It's really not that big of a deal, honest. You know my mom died when I was fourteen, after being sick for about a year. I was really close to her. Total mama's boy. Gabe went off to college the next year, dealt with things his own way. So it was just me and my Dad. My dad just threw himself into his business. I don't blame him for that, but I was a mess."

"I'm sure," I say, putting one hand on his knee, the other over my heart.

"I was just angry all the time. I was out all the time. Not with a rough crowd exactly, but they were older and they weren't the 'good kids.' I never actually messed around in school, but the principal kept picking on me, even though he knew my mom had died. And I just kept getting more and more angry. Drinking and fucking around. And one day after school, I was in a corner store with my friends. This asshole who was pissed at me because the girl he liked was into me, he kept taunting me. He was like, 'aww, why don't you go cry to your mommy—*oh wait, you can't.*' It was so stupid, but I just lost it. I punched him, and we got into a fight. I shoved him and knocked over a bunch of shelves in the store, and the shelves hit the store window, which shattered, and it was a big, loud mess.

"The guy's arm was broken and he had a black eye. But he was mostly being a spaz because he couldn't fight for shit. The owner of the store and the guy's parents pressed charges. So I was arrested when I was fifteen. That's the big awful thing. And I'm sure it set off a bunch of alarms in your ex's head, only that was the only incident. Wait, that's not exactly true. I got into a bar fight when I was twenty. But the guy was a buddy of mine, and we were both being drunk idiots. So it wasn't a big deal; it was just stupid. Other than that, I used to sleep around a lot. But you knew that."

"Wait, but were you...incarcerated?"

I can tell he's trying not to laugh at my choice of words. "No. I was not incarcerated. I mean, I was *detained* after I was arrested. The judge was pretty understanding of my situation, so I was sentenced to community service and probation and mandatory anger management counseling. My dad had to pay the kid's medical bills. And to fix up the store. I paid him back as soon as I started making money from bucket drumming."

"Were you afraid to tell me about all that?"

"No. I'm not exactly proud of it. It's just not something that usually comes up in conversation. I didn't go to jail. I don't have a record. I could run for public office if I wanted to. And after Charlie was born, I stopped drinking so much. After Clara left, I started seeing Dr. Glass again. Regularly for a while. Because I wanted to make sure I never snapped at him if I was in a mood. And I haven't."

"So you have a therapist?"

"The social worker I started seeing when I was fifteen. She eventually got another degree and started a private practice. She's cool. You'd like her. I don't always agree with her. At least, I don't always take her advice. I hardly ever take her advice actually, but..." He looks at me and sucks in a sharp breath. "I have never physically hurt anyone since that bar fight, and I would never, *ever* hurt you. You have to believe me."

"I do."

"Do you? Because I need you to."

I nod. "I trust you... How many walls have you punched?" I say it without sounding accusatory.

"Well. I've smashed a few inanimate objects over the years, and I am not proud of that. I'm not perfect. I'm not trying to be. It's like those Rumi poems you gave me. I'm just trying to have the feelings and use my feeling words, and all that...crap."

I laugh.

"I do like Dr. Glass, but I hate therapy, I really do. I just want to be able to deal with my anger in a way that doesn't hurt anybody. Or things."

I put my hand on his face.

"Does that change anything for you?" he asks, sounding so vulnerable it makes me want to bake cookies for him immediately.

I shake my head and kiss him. "Lucky for you, I've spent a lot of my life with a secret crush on Dallas Winston."

"Thank God." He kisses me back. "Wait—*who?*"

"He's a character from *The Outsiders*. You must have read it in school."

"Wait—he's the one who was an actual criminal who was in gangs."

"Well, I'm not literally comparing you to him. It's

just... Okay, if I'm being honest, it was more Matt Dillon from the movie."

"Matt Dillon? You could run into him like at any time around New York. I always see him around."

"You do...? Wait, are you jealous of my crush on early-eighties Matt Dillon?"

"No. Maybe. I don't want anyone else touching you."

"I don't want anyone else touching *you*." I kiss him again.

He starts to pull my top off.

"Wait, wait." I kiss him three more times and then stop. "I have to ask one more thing."

He says nothing. Just waits for it while staring hungrily at my mouth.

"Do you really think it was fate that we met?"

"Well, I've never been this lucky. And my karma can't be *that* great."

I wrap my arms around him and hold him so tight.

I feel so much love and desire for him, I have to check the skin on my arms because it feels like it should be oozing out of me. I can't possibly contain it all. Immediately following this rush of love is a fear that makes me ashamed. I feel ashamed that I can't get past the fear. I'm angry at myself, my first boyfriend, at Sadie and Russell for doubting that what I have with Vince is anything more than a rebound. He deserves so much pure love, and I want to give it to him, but what I have right now is a potent cocktail of emotions. If I cut myself, I am certain that my blood would be bright blue, the color of the Adios Motherfucker he made me that first night. The fact that I have even had that thought terrifies me and my whole body is shivering.

"Nina," he says, rubbing my arms. He rests his forehead against mine. "Nina, I—"

I cover his lips with mine and kiss him.

No more words.

I can't take any more.

*D*r. Glass doesn't seem anywhere near as surprised as I am that I called to schedule an appointment ASAP once I got back home.

"So, I decided to keep seeing Nina. The ex-fiancée of the guy that Sadie's been dating."

She nods once and blinks, but this is also no surprise to her. "How's that going?"

"It's good, actually. Really good. It might even be great..." I have this huge grin on my face that probably looks idiotic and my knee's bouncing up and down like it always does when I'm here. "I had a talk with my dad last night. About wanting to become a partner someday. At his firm."

She smiles and makes a note. "That is quite significant."

"I know. It means more training. Then I'd be Senior VP and then partner. I used to want to keep my options open, you know? In case some other career opportunity came along that was more interesting to me. But now

I'm not afraid to go all-in with the family business. Especially if it means more money. Even if it means more responsibility." I have to take a breath before I continue, but I look up at Dr. Glass, and I know she knows what I'm going to say next. "I want to be able to provide for someone someday. Not someone. Nina. Just her. I'm in love with her. I'm so fucking head-over-heels in love with her, I just... Sorry."

"You don't have to apologize for swearing. Especially in that context. Have you told her how you feel?"

"Not in so many words. I almost did. I want to. I don't want to scare her off."

"I'm sure that wouldn't be an issue. Being told 'I love you' tends to be a pleasant experience for most well-adjusted women. And Nina sounds like a very stable person."

"She is. Definitely. She's all the good things. You don't think things are happening too fast?"

"I didn't say that... Regardless... All in good time. It's lovely to see you feeling this way. I'm happy for you."

"I like feeling this way. I do. But I also hate it."

"How so?"

"I mean, you know me. I'm a confident guy."

"Sure."

"And it's not that she makes me feel insecure; it's just that I feel like I need to be better for her. But I might not get the chance."

"Why wouldn't you get the chance?" She slowly leans forward, trying not to appear too excited about where this conversation is going. I can tell.

"Because. Like an idiot, I told her at first that we should just spend the summer together. You know. A summer rebound. Two months seemed like a long time to commit to something that was obviously a bad idea."

"And now?"

"Now I keep looking at the calendar, and it's like each day that we get closer to each other, we're also getting closer to the end. I feel like time's running out."

"I see." She is scribbling madly in her notebook. "Vince... Can you think of another situation in your life when you felt like time was running out with someone you loved?"

I roll my eyes, even though this thought—that thought has been there. Some ghost that I've learned to live with and stay two steps ahead of. But for the past couple of months, it has slowly been catching up to me. And it's up to me to finally stop and turn around and face it. "You mean when my mom was dying?" I say, scoffing. "It is so not the same thing. Not even close. Why would you say that?"

Okay, so today is not the day for me to face it.

"Perhaps I misspoke. I don't mean that the situation is the same. But the feelings that are coming up..."

I wince.

"Do you see how this is an abandonment issue?"

I don't answer her. If this is supposed to be an *aha* moment, it's pretty underwhelming.

She sighs and continues. "Vince, we all have abandonment issues to some degree. We all have different coping mechanisms for dealing with loss. Being in a serious relationship brings up all of our feelings, all of our issues, and it's not a bad thing. They have to come up so that we can recognize them and deal with them. Sometimes, we even subconsciously create situations that will move this process along. But we need to find an effective way of dealing with them. Even when you're happy. *Especially* when you're happy. So we can ensure that you have the proper tools for when you get...*not* happy."

Not happy. This is what she gets paid two hundred bucks per forty-five minutes for.

"Please let me help you find what works for you. I can give you this early morning slot if you'd like. We could do once a week—but I recommend twice a week to start. Because things tend to get stirred up."

Decent sales pitch. Cut to the chase. Clear call to action. Not too pushy... I drop my head back and groan like Charlie when it's bedtime. What a fucking drag.

But I will do this. I will do this for Nina. At this point, it's pretty much the grandest gesture I can make, and it will be so boring. It will suck ass, and she probably won't even know I'm doing it for her.

But I'm gonna. I'm gonna get those proper tools for when I get *not* happy. Even though it's hard to believe I'll ever be *not happy* again.

"Yeah," I say to Dr. Glass with mild enthusiasm. "Let's do this. I'll take this slot. Twice a week. To start."

Chapter Twenty-Five

NINA

"It sounds like a French movie," Marnie says, almost out of breath. "One I'd actually want to watch."

"Well, it wasn't like that at all. It was more like an indie horror film."

"Did Russell show you his tattoo?"

Marnie is entirely too obsessed with this, and I really shouldn't have told her. But who else can I talk to about this? Also, we're out for a morning jog, and she promised we could stop for gelato if I tell her what I so clearly did not want to tell her about the weekend getaway.

"Of course not. I'd really rather not see Russell's private tattoo."

"Obviously we have to listen to every Amy Winehouse song and figure out what line it is."

"Marn. Promise me you won't tell anyone at school about any of this."

"*Please.* Have you ever heard me gossip about anything with anyone other than you?"

"No. *Oh my God,* it's so humid. Can we take a break?"

"Yeah. For one minute only."

We slow down to pace around and replenish fluids at an intersection.

"What does Sadie look like, though? Because now I'm picturing like, a young blonde Angelina Jolie."

I love Marnie, but I glare at her.

"Sorry. I'm sure you're way more beautiful—that goes without saying."

"She's like the shark in *Jaws.* At first, she was just this scary unknown thing lurking beneath the surface, and now she's bigger and scarier than I'd ever imagined."

"Ugh. You're gonna need a bigger boat."

"Exactly."

"Aww, honey. But you guys are in love. That's the biggest boat there is."

"I don't know if *we* are."

"*You* are."

"I'm so in love with him," I whisper, like I'm admitting defeat. "I'm a total basket case."

I shake my head, glancing across the street...and suddenly, I can't breathe.

"What?" Marnie follows my gaze.

I bolt over behind the entrance to the store on our corner, already drowning in adrenaline and cortisol. I wave Marnie over in a panic.

"*Wha*t? What is happening?"

I shush her. Vince is unlocking the door to an empty

restaurant space across the street, and Sadie is standing next to him. I can't speak.

"Oh fuck—is that Vince? Oh shit—is that *Jaws*?"

I cover my mouth. I may throw up. I peek around and see Vince go into the restaurant. Sadie follows him.

Marnie steps out, hands on her hips, staring across the street. "Honey, honey... Come on. This doesn't mean anything. She probably just showed up and he can't get rid of her."

"Can you see them? Can you see inside?"

"No. The door's closed and the windows are papered-over most of the way." She shakes her head. "This is dumb. You're getting all worked up and it's probably nothing. Let's go over there."

"I can't move. I can't breathe."

"Honey." She comes over to rub my back. "Come on. In. Out. In. Out." She reminds me how to inhale and exhale. "Good girl. You got it. Sweetie, I hate to see you like this."

"I knew this was going to happen." I bend forward to rest my hands on my knees. "I knew it."

"Okay—I'll go look first."

"Marnie, no!" I hiss.

Too late.

I watch her jog across the street and slink up between the front door and window of the restuarant, peering inside through the glass of the door. When I see how quickly she jerks her head back, when I see the look on her face, I want to die. The tightness in my chest is unbearable. The only thing worse is the feeling in my stomach. She jogs back and grabs my arm. "Let's go."

"Just tell me."

"It's not what you think."

"Marnie—just *tell* me."

"Let's go over here..." She drags me along. When we get about a block away in the opposite direction, she pulls me around the corner and pulls no punches: "She was trying to kiss him. But he was resisting her. I promise you, he was totally resisting her and pushing her away. She was all over him, but he was pushing her away and *that's* what matters. Look at me, honey. Look at me."

I somehow manage to lift my eyes to her concerned face. It's the same face she has when one of her kids or students has fallen down. She's not denying that it might hurt, but she doesn't want to make it worse by freaking out.

"It's okay," she says. "I would tell you if I thought it looked like he was into it, and he was not. Definitely not. I'm sure he will tell you about it later and you'll both laugh about what a little drama queen you were about absolutely nothing."

I try to concentrate on Marnie's face. I do trust her. I don't trust Sadie. But right now I don't know if I trust Vince, and that's what's killing me.

I TOLD VINCE THAT I WAS TOO TIRED TO DO anything last night, which was certainly true. But I was mostly exhausted from crying so much. I am fully aware that this is about six years' worth of tears that I have to get out of my system and only some of it has to do with Vince. But I got no sleep. I'm exhausted.

I've agreed to meet him for lunch at the Italian restaurant where I gave him the Rumi book. I didn't want him to come to my apartment. There are too many places he could kiss me there, and it would make me lose my resolve.

I can control a room full of six-year-olds. It should be so much easier for me to control my own brain. But I can't. Not since I first laid eyes on Vince Devlin.

My eyes have puffy gray bags under them today. There isn't enough concealer in the world to hide them or enough lip gloss to detract from them. All I can do is wear sunglasses and hope that I don't burst into tears and shoot snot out of my nose as soon as I see him.

I get to the restaurant five minutes earlier than our agreed-upon time so I can get settled and calm myself down.

Un, deux, trois—fuck.

He got here before me. The hostess points in his direction. He's sitting at a corner table on the patio. He looks nervous. Nervous and beautiful and completely capable of destroying my heart with one look.

He sees me and smiles, stands up. I let him kiss my cheek and hold out my chair for me. When I sit down, a small, sad sigh escapes me.

"Hey you," he says. "I missed you yesterday."

I don't remove my sunglasses because I'm already tearing up. I nod. "I missed you too." The words come out soft and gravelly.

"Are you getting a cold?"

"Maybe."

"You should get their minestrone soup." He looks so worried about me. It's too sweet. He rubs his lips together. I have this feeling he needs to tell me something, and I just want him to get it over with.

"I just saw my dad. He said that Charlie wants me to tell you that book was a big hit with his girlfriend."

"She's not his girlfriend," I whisper.

"She will be soon enough. He's a Devlin." He grins.

I shift around in my chair.

"You gonna take your sunglasses off?"

"Not yet."

"Are you okay?"

I take a breath. "How've you been? How was your day yesterday?"

"Weird."

"Yeah?"

"Yeah. I had so many calls about a property that I just listed. More than I was expecting."

"Oh yeah? Did you...have showings? At the property?"

"Yeah. What'd you get up to? I missed you. I told you that."

Our waitress comes to take our order, but I haven't looked at the menu yet. He orders me a minestrone soup and hot tea. He's being so sweet, it's terrible. When the waitress leaves, he reaches across the table to pull my sunglasses off my face.

"Whoa." He stares at my pink, swollen, damp eyes.

I can't look at him anymore.

"Shit," he says under his breath. "What is it?"

"Umm..." I wipe away a tear. There's no one seated immediately around us and no reason to put off this conversation. I stare at the center of the table as I speak. "I've been thinking... We should have a little time-out. Take a break. I just need to be on my own for a little bit to sort through my feelings. And I don't want to speak for you, but maybe you could do the same."

"Why would we do that?"

"It's not you, Vince. I promise. It's just...difficult to overcome the circumstances in which we met."

"I don't see why it matters how we met. You met your principal the normal boring way, and look how *that* turned out."

Always the great debater.

"I just think we should take a break before things get too serious."

He is quiet for a long time before saying, "Well then, darlin'...you are way too late." I finally glance up at him, and the look he gives me breaks my heart in two, but it wasn't the stoic one I was expecting. *He* looks heartbroken. "Why is this happening?"

"Vince...it was bound to happen eventually, you know that."

"Why is this happening *now*?"

"I saw you. Yesterday morning. With Sadie."

He doesn't even blink. "*Nothing* happened. I mean, she was trying something, but I didn't... You don't trust me?"

"Were you going to tell me that you saw her?"

"No, Nina. That's not what I was going to tell you today. I don't give a fuck about Sadie—I've had so much on my mind that seeing her barely even registered in my brain. This can't be about that."

"Well, I do give a fuck about Sadie. And about

Russell, and about you. And I want to be able to only give a fuck about you and me. But I need some time on my own so I can think about everything that's happened. It's a lot, Vince. It was fast."

"You said you aren't mad at him anymore."

"I'm not, but I never had time to process the breakup either. I was with him for three years. I was engaged to him. I may not have been in love with him, but it mattered."

Our of the corner of my eye, I see the waitress heading toward us with my soup and tea, but as soon as she catches our body language, she turns on her heels, pretending to have forgotten something, and goes back inside.

"Are you telling me you still have feelings for him? Is that why you're worried about me and Sadie—you're projecting?"

"I don't have that kind of feelings for him. No. God, no. Vince—I'm a mess right now. School starts in less than three weeks, and I can't be an emotional mess when I'm responsible for dozens of small children. Why don't you understand this?"

"You said you'd give me the whole summer." It's an accusation, the way he says it. He's getting aggressive, and I'm getting defensive. I honestly didn't expect him to be like this. He's usually so open and understanding. I don't know what I was thinking.

"I know. I'm sorry. I'm not good at this."

"At what? Being with me?"

"I love being with you. I just don't know if I'm good at being me when I'm with you."

"What the fuck is that supposed to mean? Who are

you being?"

"Vince."

"No, tell me. I wanna know. Who were you being? Who did I fall in love with?"

He says it so quickly, my brain doesn't even register what that question means. "I've booked a flight. I'm going to Bloomington for ten days."

"What? When?"

"Tomorrow. I'm going to stay with my parents."

"You already planned this. Without telling me."

"I just decided to yesterday. I'm telling you now."

He shakes his head. I can visibly see him shutting down.

"Vince. I didn't mean for this to be a permanent break. I just need some space. It's not your fault, but I'm overwhelmed. If I stay here, I'll just want to keep seeing you, and it's not... I don't know what else to do."

I've lost him. I can see it in his eyes. "What about Charlie?" His voice is so cold, I actually shiver.

"Well...I can FaceTime with him when I'm gone."

He shakes his head. He won't even look at me. Whatever he's thinking about, even though he's physically still here, I can tell that he's already left me.

"We can still be friends while we're working through this. You and me. Me and Charlie. It's not like with Sadie—I'm just talking about a couple of weeks."

"No." He looks up at me. His irises are so much darker than they've ever been. I barely even recognize them.

"No?"

"We had a deal."

"I'm sorry if you perceive this as some sort of

betrayal, but I was hoping you'd be a little more flexible and understanding."

"Yeah? I was hoping a good girl like you would be a lot more reliable."

"How am I not reliable? You're the one with the history of lovin' and leavin' 'em."

"I don't know what else I could ever say or do to show you that it was different with you." He keeps shaking his head. "You get everything, or you get nothing."

"That doesn't sound so different to me."

He winces, but he's not budging. He is so stubborn. I never would have expected him to be this stubborn.

"That doesn't seem unreasonable to you, Vince?"

"You know what—don't talk to me like I'm a six-year-old. Deciding to leave town for ten days before you even give me a chance to talk about this seems unreasonable to me, yeah. It's pretty immature, too." He stands up, pulls a twenty-dollar bill out of his wallet, and drops it on the table. "You know what—forget about Charlie. My dad's started bringing Sharon around a lot. He'll be fine."

"Is there a one-woman limit in the Devlin household? What is *that* supposed to mean?"

I can see that he regrets saying that, but I'm so mad at him right now I don't care.

"You're leaving? That's it?"

"The difference with you, Nina...so we're clear...is that I *wanted* to give you everything. *You're* the one who's leaving. Deal with that."

I don't watch him walk away. I can't. I already know that even if I run after him, it is way too late.

When Marnie comes over, I literally have to crawl across the floor to buzz her in and unlock my door. Does this make me a drama queen? Perhaps. But my plan for sorting through my feelings in a way that's not overwhelming has not gotten off to a good start.

At least I don't have to force myself to feel something.

I don't need a pop or country song to remind me how to feel. I don't need alcohol to make me feel more or less of anything. I'm feeling everything and nothing. I feel Vince in every pore of my body as much as I feel his absence.

Eyes closed, I feel Marnie take my hand and place something smooth and squishy into it. I don't have to see to know that it's a Capri Sun juice pouch. This may be the last time I smile, even a little bit, for the rest of my life.

"Sit up," she says. "Drink up."

I do. It's my favorite flavor—tropical punch. A sweet reminder of what summer is supposed to taste like, instead of tears and self-loathing.

"Thank you," I say meekly. "Can I make you some tea?"

"No. I brought my shoulder to cry on again. It didn't get used at all the last time around."

The last time around. "Oh God. This is my second breakup in two months."

"Yer on a roll, kiddo."

"I spent three years in a relationship with Russell and didn't shed a tear when he dumped me. I spend just over a month with this guy, and now that it's over, I feel like something has died inside. What's wrong with me?"

"First of all, there is nothing wrong with you, sunshine. Secondly, you didn't cry for Russell because you knew exactly what you were going to get with him, and you were relieved you didn't have to keep getting that shit. It's sad about Vince because you had a glimpse of how great it could be, and you're never going to see it come to fruition. And that sucks. It feels like you're dying inside because your lady parts are never going to rub up against that beautiful man's body or sweet mouth ever again."

"Marnie!"

"Sorry."

"Oh my God. It's true. He told me he fell in love with me, and I didn't even respond. It was so unexpected. He must hate me."

"No."

"Yes. Whether he was into it with Sadie the other day or not, I probably just drove him back to her."

"No. No way."

"Ugh. I *hate* me. I can't believe I blew it."

"Honey. You were trying to protect yourself. We all do that."

"I've been trying to protect myself my whole life, and the only time I've ever been really happy was when I stopped doing that."

"It takes a lot of practice to get used to a change like that. It's like learning to ride a bike without the training wheels. Maybe next time you'll get the hang of it. Find that balance."

If I weren't too tired to cry anymore, that would send me into another humiliating fit of sobs. "I don't want a next time with someone else," I whisper.

"It might not be with someone else." She rubs my back. "I mean, I'm no shrink, but it seems to me that you're both pretty similar in really important ways."

Sniff. "You mean sexually?"

"Well. Sure. But also emotionally. You both have abandonment issues."

"What? No we don't. We aren't needy. I mean, I'm not. He's *definitely* not."

"It goes the other way too. Emotional distance. Sound familiar?"

I stare at Marnie for an eternity. How did I not realize what a genius she is? "Dave is the luckiest guy alive."

She scoffs. "Oh, I am not this understanding with my husband. He's wrong about everything. He's just lucky I stick around long enough to fall in love with him over and over again." She holds out her hand. I take it and squeeze her hand with more gratitude than I could show with words. "You'll have that one day too, honey. I know you will."

———

To further illustrate my poor judgment when deciding to come to Bloomington for ten days in August —it has been so humid that when I cry outside on the back porch, my tears never evaporate. They basically turn to gel and stick to my face.

My parents, strangely, haven't been as worried about me as they were several years ago. Maybe it's because I'm not depressed. I've just been so, so sad. Or maybe it's because my dad has finally figured out how to get his hair to look awesome with the putty that Vince recommended. And that makes both him and my mom too happy to worry about their lovesick daughter.

Or maybe they've noticed that I'm actually starting to get better, even though I haven't communicated with Vince at all since seeing him at the restaurant.

The space that I thought I needed in order to sort through my feelings has somehow only been filled with more love for Vince. It's a cruel joke. Returning to Bloomington a few years after leaving because I didn't want to be reminded of my first broken heart. And now, trying to escape Brooklyn in order to avoid running into my second broken heart. But there is a difference.

Probably without planning it, Vince has broken my heart wide open.

I may have lost him. He might stay mad at me forever. I might never see him again. I may still be mad at him for being so stubborn. But I love *love* again. I get why people fall in love, even if the relationship doesn't last. We don't dread the summer just because we know it doesn't last forever. We revel in it. I will never regret one second that I spent with Vince. Every single word, kiss, look, feeling, moment that he gave me in the span of weeks will live in me for a lifetime.

The mess we made really is more beautiful than anything I've ever known.

I've never really understood why people get tattoos before, but now I just want—now I need—to have something permanent on my body. To show how I feel on the inside. To show that it won't change, even when circumstances have. To prove that even though it might hurt at first...what remains will be something that I've chosen to define who I am and what matters to me.

Chapter Twenty-Seven

VINCE

"Can you tell me how you're feeling right now, Vince?"

Shit, I almost forgot where I was. I just zoned out. I basically just paid sixteen dollars and sixty-five cents for my therapist to stare at me for three minutes.

"I was just thinking about Charlie" is what I say. *Yeah. I know. I told you what I'm thinking about instead of how I'm feeling, Dr. Glass.*

She gives me this look. I know that look. She thinks I'm regressing. I'm not regressing.

"You think I'm regressing, don't you?"

"Do *you* think you're regressing?"

Obviously, I'm going to ignore *that* bullshit question completely. "Charlie asked when we get to hang out with Nina again."

"What did you tell him?"

"I told him she's visiting her parents out of town. When he asked if we could FaceTime her, I told him she doesn't get good cell phone reception over there. Which might be a lie, I don't know. I felt bad about that. I just didn't want to tell him he might not see her again. Anyway, he asked me to show him where she is. On a map. He's got this map of the US on his wall because he's a nerd. And he sticks push pins into the places he wants to go visit. I pointed to Indiana, but the map only has Ft. Wayne and Indianapolis on it, and I don't even know where the fuck Bloomington, Indiana is... Sorry."

She blinks and doesn't say anything. Because she's told me a million times that I don't have to apologize for swearing in here, but I always apologize anyway.

"Anyway, he stuck a green pin in the center of the state of Indiana. Because green means go. He wants to go there. And all I could think was that I should go there. Find Nina. Tell her I love her. Tell her I'm sorry. Tell her everything she means to me. And then I thought about my appointments with you. And how I'm doing this for her. And after a while, instead of having that panicky feeling that I need to go to her and *do* something to show her I'm worthy of...her. Like just show up and grab her and fuck her until we're both too tired to remember all this shit we've... Sorry... Instead, I felt..."

Dr. Glass might slide off her chair if she leans forward any more. "Yes?"

"I could feel her inside me. In my fucking *heart*, okay? Jesus, that is so cheesy. But it didn't even matter all that much that she's in Indiana, because I still feel connected to her. Fuck, that is corny as fuck."

"It's not corny, Vince," she says while scribbling in her notebook, and I'm pretty sure I can see her drawing hearts and check marks.

Yay for fucking me.

I don't even wait for her to ask me to *go on*. "I was feeling really mad before that. At myself. At first, I was mad at her for leaving. And then I felt guilty for being mad at her because it's my fault."

"It's not your fault, Vince."

"Okay. If you're gonna pull that *Good Will Hunting* 'It's not your fault' shit with me and try to hug me until I cry, I'm leaving."

She purses her lips, trying not to smile or laugh at me. "I promise not to do that. But it's not your fault if Nina doesn't trust you. That's her thing. Not yours."

"Well, how the fuck do you decide what's yours and what's hers if you're in a relationship?"

"That's a very good question, and that's one of the things I'd like to work on. We all need to find a way to be our own separate person while we're in a healthy relationship with someone else. It's not easy. But self-acceptance is a good place to start."

"I accept myself. I'm fucking awesome all the time."

"Well, good for fucking you, Vince. I guess my work here is done, then."

It takes us both a couple of seconds to realize what she just said.

She purses her lips again. "Sorry."

"You don't have to apologize for swearing if it's in that context," I assure her in the same tone she usually uses with me.

And then we both laugh. I don't think I've ever laughed in here before. I'm not even sure if people are allowed to laugh in therapy. Are we breaking a rule or something?

When we finally stop laughing, she just watches me and waits for me to say what comes next. And all I can say right now is, "I miss my mom."

"I know. I'm sorry."

"I'm not gonna cry."

"You don't have to. But it's okay if you do."

I check my watch. Only fifteen minutes left in this session. Whenever I get here, it seems impossible that I'll be able to talk for forty-five minutes, and by the end I'm never ready for it to be over. "I know I only have this slot booked for two days a week, but..."

"If you need to see me more than that right now, I will find a way to work it into my schedule. If you promise to come to the sessions."

"Yeah. I will." I try to formulate the right sentence in my head before opening my mouth again. Me words. Feeling words. What do I want? Blah fucking blah, whatever. "I'm afraid that I'll lose Nina if I don't do something. To show her that I care. I'm not gonna obsess about it, but I want to do something."

"Why don't you send her a brief text? You said she had hoped to stay friends during this break."

"Yeah. Before I fucked things up."

"Let's try to reframe that, shall we?"

"Before I created yet another fucked-up situation to deal with?"

"Moving on—why don't you send Nina a brief text.

Just to let her know that you're thinking about her. That it's not over for you."

"I don't know if I can be brief. And I don't know if I'm ready to have a big conversation with her. Or if she's ready for it."

"Sometimes, the best thing to say to someone else is the thing that you most need to hear... This can be your homework assignment."

It is impossible not to roll my eyes at that.

"Think about what you most wish someone in your life—from your present or past—could say to you. And then text it to Nina. If it feels right."

I let my head fall back and groan, rubbing my eyes. This is so lame.

"I'm very proud of you, Vince. This was good. I trust that you'll do the right thing."

"Stop trying to make me cry, Dr. G."

"Okay."

I've thought about it all day, but I finally know what I want to say to Nina. I'm not going to be the guy who tells a woman "I love you" for the first time ever in a text message. I'm not going to steal from some dead mystical poet, even though he was able to articulate everything I've been feeling for her since the day I first saw her. So I type out:

Hi. You don't have to write back. I just want to tell you, Nina...

. . .

AND THEN I SAY THE SIMPLE THINGS THAT I'VE needed to hear for fourteen years:

I'M STILL HERE FOR YOU. YOU ARE NOT FORGOTTEN. We're gonna be okay. I will see you again.

Chapter Twenty-Eight

NINA

And before I know it, it's the first day of school. I've got my classroom all decorated, I've got my **Hello, I'm Miss Parks** name tag on. My name is on the chalkboard, my lesson plans for the first week are fully planned out, my teaching supplies are organized, my classroom rules are ready to be explained in a clear and fun manner. I haven't said a real swear word out loud in two weeks, and I haven't cried in over a week.

When I did cry those last few times, it was tears of joy, because Vince Devlin is wonderful. Because he somehow managed to text me the exact thing I needed to hear. And after staring at that text for half an hour, I finally replied with a heart emoji.

I don't even regret it. Because we will see each other again, and there will be more time for all the words. The good words. The good bad words. The great bad decisions. I trust that.

Beside every thought I have about vowels and fractions and the pros and cons of hand sanitizer are two thoughts about Vince. But they're just there keeping me company; they don't send me into a tizzy. See, I use words like "tizzy." I'm officially a dorky first-grade teacher again.

One of the things I thought about when I was getting back into teacher mode was how thrilling it is to be around a six-year-old's enthusiasm for life. Sometimes that enthusiasm causes them to bite off more than they can chew, and I watch them get disappointed and upset when their extremely high expectations don't get fulfilled. They crash and burn, getting exhausted after bursts of energy and effort. And it's my job to help them reach their lofty goals by breaking them down into manageable parts so they don't get disheartened and give up altogether.

I'm finally helping myself in the same way. Today, I'll be grateful that I got to experience falling in love— twice. Tomorrow, I'll wake up and be excited because I can feel that love whenever I want to.

I still haven't heard from Vince since Indiana, and I haven't reached out to him yet. I plan to, next weekend. Once the first week of school is behind me. Until then, we're okay.

I've seen Russell in passing twice. He seems okay, although if he *weren't* okay, he wouldn't show it. We had a quick conversation about telling our co-workers that we're no longer a couple, but only if they ask. We aren't going to make a big announcement or anything. He didn't say anything about whether he's still with Sadie or not, and he didn't ask me about Vince. I really think that on that front, for Russell and me, we'll be fine.

I'm standing at the door to my classroom, waiting to

greet my new students, when I look across the hall and see Tyler's mom pass by the entrance from the big yard, looking around. My kids haven't started to arrive yet, so I hurry over to the doors.

"Eve?"

"Oh, thank God." She approaches. "I was hoping I'd catch you."

"Hi. Everything okay?"

"Oh yeah. I just dropped Tyler off."

"Oh good. Whose class is he in?"

"Mrs. Yee."

"That's great—she's wonderful."

"Yeah, she seems cool."

We stare at each other for a second.

"So, you all had a good summer?" I ask.

"Yeah, really good. You?"

I smile. "It was the best." Sighing, I finally ask the question I've wanted to ask ever since I spotted her: "How is he?"

She lets out a long exhale and puts her hands on her hips. "He's...okay? I think. It's so hard to tell with him. I mean, it was rough for a couple of days there. I was really worried about him. It seemed like he wasn't sleeping, and I guess he drank a lot that first night after you...whatever...but...he's been seeing his therapist a few times a week, and I think..."

She notices my eyes widen and realizes this might be news to me.

"I mean. It's not my place to say this, but..."

"Yeah, sure. I'm sure you're busy."

"But I think you guys should talk."

"Oh."

"Like, soon."

"Oh. Okay." *Oh...okay*.

A horde of parents and five- and six-year-olds suddenly crowds in toward us, and Eve and I get separated. I hear her say "bye" and I have so many questions but no time to think about anything other than getting backpacks into cubby holes and kids into their desks.

BY 3:20, WHEN MY CLASSROOM IS MIRACULOUSLY emptied and quiet, I start to tidy up and reorganize and pack up my things. I can finally acknowledge the butterflies in my stomach and the re-emerging tingle in my lady parts in anticipation of talking to Vince, *like soon*.

There are no messages from him on my phone.

I have a text from Marnie that says: **Staff room before home? Zonaforpthwak.**

She really needs to learn to lock her screen before sliding her phone into her pocket.

I reply with: **Heading home! Talk later.**

WHEN I'M THREE BLOCKS TOWARD HOME, COMPOSING a speech in my head, I hear a motorcycle engine approaching behind me and stop in my tracks.

Un, deux, trois, ohhh merde, please be him.

The man on the motorcycle pauses alongside me and pulls off his helmet with his strong, slightly rough, very capable hands. Seeing his beautiful face again takes my breath away.

"Hello, Miss Parks."

I have to clear my throat. "Hi."

From where I stand, his eyes look green with patches of brown and gold—the color of a summer lawn after a long day of welcome rain. I take a step toward him.

"Sorry I don't have more of a grand gesture prepared," he says with a sheepish grin that reminds me of Charlie. "I've been too busy going to therapy and working toward becoming a partner at my dad's brokerage. So I'm kind of exhausted." He shrugs. "But I'm doing it all for you."

"I feel like I've been waiting my whole life to hear someone say that."

"You want a ride home?"

I nod. "Yes. Yes I do."

"Hop on."

I put on the extra helmet and climb onto the seat behind him, hiking up my skirt. I wrap my arms around his waist, pressing my cheek against his back. He smells like a warm, musky forest that I want to run through naked and get lost in with him.

When he parks the bike in front of my building, he stays on after I climb off. He removes his helmet, runs his fingers through his hair, and says, "I didn't call you because I figured you needed to get ready for school..."

"Yeah. I didn't call you because I was getting ready for school, and...I just kind of knew we'd see each other when we were ready."

He grins.

I love that grin.

"Can I come up?"

"Yes."

He nods once. There's a clarity in his gaze that I haven't seen before. I've always felt like he could see right through me, but now I feel like I can see into him too. He locks both wheels of his bike and follows me upstairs. We don't speak or touch or look at each other, but I feel the electricity of him on my skin, all over.

As soon as we're through the door to my apartment, I drop my bag, he drops his motorcycle helmets and messenger bag, and my back is pressed up against the wall, his lips on mine, my hands all over him, and I finally feel like I'm home.

"I missed you so much," he says. "I love you so fucking much. I'm sorry I was such a dick that day."

"Vince, I'm more in love with you now than ever." He kisses my neck as he unbuttons my blouse, and all these random words and sounds pour out of my mouth, until I'm finally able to form a sentence. "I realized I'm more *me* when I'm with you than when I'm by myself or with anyone else. I'm so sorry I had to hurt you to figure that out."

"You don't have to apologize to me."

"No, I do. I have to say this—wait. Wait." I hold him away from myself so I can get the words out before my brain drowns in a bath of hormones and relief. I place one hand over my chest and one on his. "I keep thinking it's like I was hiding this hole in my heart. And you came along and revealed it to me. And then you patched it up." We are just a few feet away from that part of the wall he punched the night we met, and I know he knows what I'm talking about. "And then I broke yours. I'll never forgive myself for that..." I brace myself and wait for him to laugh at me for saying anything so corny out loud.

Instead, he says, "Baby, I would rather let you break my heart every day of my life than live without you."

I cover my mouth. "Oh my God. Vince. We're so cheesy."

He leans down, his lips hovering an inch from mine. "I think we should stop talking now."

I smile. "I have a surprise for you." I slowly push the waistband of my skirt down past my hip.

"I like it so far," he says with a smirk.

"You're going to have to be gentle with me," I say as I push the skirt down a couple more inches to reveal the tattoo I got when I was in Indiana. It's healing nicely. I think Joni Mitchell would be proud to know that her lyrics have a permanent place on my lower abdomen.

I watch his eyes light up as he reads:

Oh I could drink a case of you darling
And I would still be on my feet
I would still be on my feet

"For me?"

"For you, darling."

He tugs my skirt down so that it falls to the floor, scoops me up in his arms, and carries me to my bed, placing me down on it ever so gently. He kisses all around the tattoo and keeps staring at it when he says,

"Hey, Miss Parks—you got any big plans for the fall, or... the rest of your life?"

"Yeah," I say, reaching for him and pulling him to me. I will always, always, reach for him and pull him to me. "I've got some pretty big plans." I kiss his ear and whisper, "I know a guy."

EPILOGUE - VINCE

* Ten Months Later *

The wedding of Neil Devlin to Sharon Hale is warm and pleasant and understated, just as they wanted it to be. It's a second marriage for both of them. I am as sure that my mom would like Sharon as I am that Charlie adores her and that my dad will love and cherish her for as long as she'll put up with him. Watching him slowly give himself to her has been good for Gabe and me, as neither of us ever thought we'd see the day he'd look at any woman the way he looked at our mother.

Life does go on.

We are all, amazingly, okay.

My dad's married again. Gabe's been dating a great lady for over two months. Charlie even has a little girl-friend, as I had predicted. Russell and Sadie broke up like half a year ago, and I even sort of get along with him when we have to see each other.

As Dr. Glass would say: "All in good time."

The good times with Nina continue. But I've been waiting patiently for what feels like an eternity to get to this moment.

The wedding reception at our friend's restaurant is in full swing, and Nina looks warily at the drinks I've just made for us at the bar. I just invented this cocktail. It's big and Irish green, and it contains twelve ingredients. One for each month I've known her.

"It's called a Lucky Motherflorker," I tell her.

She laughs and takes a sip. "Hmmm... It tastes so bitter and so sweet."

"You got that right." I pull something out of my left pocket and slide it across the bar counter toward her. "This is for you."

Her eyes go wide at the sight of the little black velvet box, but she doesn't hesitate to grab it and open it. *That's my girl.*

She looks a little confused when she sees the key inside it. "But I already have a key to your place," she says.

"This is just a metaphorical hypothetical key to *our* place. A couple of months ago I told a guy I know to keep an eye open for two bedrooms in Carroll Gardens or Cobble Hill. So you can still walk to work. And there's a place about to come on the market that I want to show you tomorrow. I really think you'll like it. And I'd really like to live there with you."

She smirks.

God, I love it when she smirks.

"Well, that sounds great, but I'm not in the mood to get raped or murdered this summer."

Ahh, memories. "I promise I'll keep my hands where

you can see them. So you know exactly what they're doing to you at all times."

She giggles. "People do this? Meet in a liquor store, rebound with each other, go on a double date with their exes, and then move in together?"

"*We* do."

"Yeah. We do."

"Good." I pull another box out from my right pocket and walk out from behind the counter. It is too fucking priceless that the Beyoncé ballad she loves just happens to be playing when I get down on one knee in front of her.

I hear Eve scream from the other side of the room, and I don't even care that all my co-workers are watching me do this. All I care about is the look on Nina's amazing face.

"Thing is, I want to live there with you...as your husband. If you're open to that."

"I am. I am very open to that."

"You'll marry me?"

"Oh. Hell. Yes." She pulls me up off the floor— because that's what she does, she pulls me up—takes the ring, and slides it onto her perfect finger. "Vince Devlin," she says, kissing my cheek and saying into my ear, "I'm gonna marry the *fuck* out of you."

And that's how I know it's summer again, and that for us, it always will be.

AUTHOR'S NOTES

Quote from the song "A Case of You" by Joni Mitchell from the album *Blue*.

Quote from *The minute I heard my first love story...* by Rumi, translation by Coleman Barks in *The Essential Rumi*.

ALSO BY KAYLEY LORING

All of my books are available in Kindle Unlimited!

SLEEPER (Shane and Willa's story) – available in audio

CHARMER (Nico and Kat's story) – coming to audio

(The New York/Brooklyn standalones)

REBOUND WITH ME (Vince and Nina) - coming to audio summer 2020

COME BACK TO BED (Matt and Bernadette) - available in audio

TONIGHT YOU'RE MINE (Chase and Aimee) - available in audio

THE PLUS ONES (Keaton and Roxy) - available in audio

BACK FOR MORE (Wes and Lily) – available in audio

HELLO DARLING (Evan and Stella) – coming to audio summer 2020

SEXY NERD (John and Olivia)

EVERY INCH OF YOU (Brad and Vivian)

The Work Less/Play More series of standalones

Printed in Great Britain
by Amazon